the COSMIC ATLAS of ALFIE FLEET

the COSMIC ATLAS of ALFIE FLEET

MARTIN HOWARD
illustrated by CHRIS MOULD

OXFORD
UNIVERSITY PRESS

OXFORD
UNIVERSITY PRESS

Great Clarendon Street, Oxford OX2 6DP

Oxford University Press is a department of the University of Oxford.
It furthers the University's objective of excellence in research, scholarship,
and education by publishing worldwide. Oxford is a registered trade mark of
Oxford University Press in the UK and in certain other countries

Text copyright © Martin Howard 2019
Illustrations copyright © Chris Mould 2019

The moral rights of the author have been asserted

First published 2019

Database right Oxford University Press (maker)

British Library Cataloguing in Publication Data
Data available

ISBN: 978-0-19-276750-9

1 3 5 7 9 10 8 6 4 2

Printed in India

Paper used in the production of this book is a natural,
recyclable product made from wood grown in sustainable forests.
The manufacturing process conforms to the environmental
regulations of the country of origin.

FOR MAIA, BUFFY
AND SAM

– M.H.

THE FOOT SPA PROBLEM

There were a lot of miserable things about being poor, Alfie Fleet told himself. Taking freezing cold showers in the middle of winter was pretty rubbish. Wearing clothes so patched that homeless people sometimes slipped a few pennies into his hand was embarrassing. The diet of fish soup, made from offcuts his mother brought home from work, wasn't his idea of a good time either. The heads always glared up at him as if it was all his fault.

The worst thing about being poor though was, of course, never having enough money and—as we join him—Alfie Fleet was especially miserable about not having enough money.

Let's pause there. Before we get into his money problems we'll take a moment to get to know Alfie Fleet a bit better. We will—after all—be travelling to the ends of the universe with him.

He is a boy. That much is obvious from the odd shape of him. Alfie looks like he was assembled from sticks and string, with knees and elbows glued on at random, as is often the way with boys. He is not especially handsome, but neither is he hideous. It is unlikely that anyone would want to hide his freckled, sandy-haired head with, say, a paper bag. He's a fairly normal boy: trips over his own feet a lot; not too fussy about trimming his toenails or keeping his ears clean. A boy.

He lives in a tiny flat in a big city, which he shares with his mother. Despite the passing trains that make its windows rattle and the dripping taps and pipes that bang unexpectedly in the middle of the night, their home is always neat. Keeping it tidy is easy. Alfie and his mother don't own much stuff to make a mess with: a couple of lumpy beds; a sagging tartan sofa that gives them headaches if they look at it too long; a leaky fridge that tries hard but never keeps anything cold; an oven that may or may not cook depending on its mood; and a radio that pops and crackles like breakfast cereal. That's pretty much it. The reason they are so poor is that Alfie's dad stole his mum's heart and then her credit card, before running off with that Julie from number sixteen. He left Alfie's mother with a mountain of debt she is still struggling to pay off, and Alfie himself. Although his mum often tells him she wouldn't change a thing, sometimes Alfie hears her crying over bills through the paper-thin walls.

We join him at the kitchen table, which had a folded up wedge of cardboard stuffed under one leg to stop it wobbling and was half in the kitchen and half in the lounge because the flat was that small. He was pretending to read a book . . .

Alfie's mum stepped out of her bedroom wearing a dressing gown. As always, she looked tired and smelt of fish.

That was another thing about being poor, Alfie told himself. However much his mum scrubbed, she could never truly get rid of the smell that came with working at the fish market.

'Morning, son,' she said, sleepily. 'What's today's book?'

'Jarvis O'Toole's new one, *The Dragonsong of Flame*,' Alfie replied, lifting his library book to show her the cover. He did it carefully, so that she couldn't see what was hidden between its pages.

'Any good bum jokes?'

'It's not really that sort of book,' Alfie said. 'Oh, I made you a cup of tea,' he added, nodding at the steaming mug.

Alfie's mum took a sip and leant against the fridge, which—as usual—was slightly warmer than the rest of the flat. 'No bum jokes? Sounds awful,' she replied. Alfie's mum liked a good bum joke. She had that kind of sense of humour. 'I'm off to work in a minute. There's fish soup in the pan for your lunch.'

Alfie forced himself to grin. 'Delicious,' he said.

'Alfie, my boy,' his mum replied, 'you're a good lad but you're a terrible liar. Sorry, fish soup is all we've got.'

'On the plus side, I think I saw a prawn in it,' said Alfie. He liked prawns, which isn't to say he'd go on holiday with one, but at least they didn't glare at him.

'It's payday tomorrow. And my birthday. Special treat, we're going to Mr Ulcer's Pie Shop for pie and chips,' his mum replied.

'I've gone off pie and chips,' said Alfie, who loved pie and chips.

'Again—terrible liar,' said his mum, raising an eyebrow.

'No, seriously. Give *yourself* a treat instead,' Alfie shot back. 'Go and see that new Johnny Nicebutt movie. You *like* Johnny Nicebutt.'

'His name is Johnny Nesbitt, as you know perfectly well,' Alfie's mum sighed, leaning over to ruffle his hair. 'Although he does have a very nice butt. But come on, it's *pie*. And it's my birthday. Mr Ulcer said he'd put a candle in it for me. Is it a date?'

'I dunno,' said Alfie. 'I'd still rather you bought yourself something.'

'Well you can't have everything you want,' his mum replied. 'If you haven't worked that out by now, you're not paying enough attention. So, it's a date then?'

'It's a date,' said Alfie, with a sigh.

'Birthday pie with my boy. Just what I always wanted.' Alfie's mum smiled.

'Living the dream, Mum. Living the dream.'

'So, what are you doing today?' his mum asked, looking slightly guilty. Alfie knew she hated leaving him alone during the school holidays.

'Oh, you know, the usual. Thought I'd just stay in and read. Quiet day.' Alfie held his book up again. This time he lied brilliantly, proving his mum completely wrong about his lying abilities. Although he was playing it cool, beneath his calm exterior he was a desperate boy. He didn't have an actual plan for the day at that exact moment, but a plan was called for and it wouldn't include sitting around with Jarvis O'Toole's latest bestseller.

His mum nodded. 'OK, try and get some fresh air, too.'

'In *this* city? What fresh air?'

'And some exercise,' his mum insisted. 'Go and jump over dog poos in the park.'

'All right, if it makes you happy. I'll take the rubbish down, too, and make the beds, so you can put your feet up when you get home. Do you want a Fancy Goat Crumble rematch tonight?'

A short explanation is needed here. As Alfie's mum couldn't afford a television or tablets or video games, she and her son usually spent their evenings playing the weirdest second-hand board games they could find in the bargain bins of the local charity shops. Fancy Goat Crumble was their latest favourite, though some of the goats' beards were missing. This may not sound like a lot of fun but in actual fact they spent a lot more time laughing than most people.

'You bet I do,' chuckled Alfie's mum. 'I still can't believe you crumbled my goat last night.'

'It's all in the strategy,' said Alfie, with a wink.

His mum glanced at her watch. 'Rats, I'm going to be late. I'd better get dressed. Will you be all right?'

'I'll be fine,' replied Alfie, nodding at his book.

As her bedroom door closed, Alfie sighed with relief. She hadn't spotted that he had been hiding a magazine called *Investment Today* between the pages of the Jarvis O'Toole novel, or that hidden between the pages of *Investment Today*—like a riddle wrapped inside an enigma—was a small but colourful brochure for the Sole Sensation 6000 Foot Spa, with Soothejet Technology and Vibrating Toe-Polishers. Across the top of the brochure were printed the words 'Treat Your Feet!' in bold letters. Beneath them, in slightly smaller letters, it said: 'Only £149.99!'

Alfie stuffed it into his backpack and studied the front cover of *Investment Today*. It said: 'STOCK MARKET SLOWS DOWN.'

Here, we arrive at the nub, crux, or heart of Alfie's money problem. His mum's birthday was the following day, and he wanted to buy her something

special: a Sole Sensation 6000 Foot Spa, in fact.
For twelve to fourteen hours every day she stood
at a bench gutting fish, and her feet played her up
something dreadful. A Sole Sensation 6000 Foot Spa
would be the perfect gift and Alfie was determined
that she would have one. As he was not the kind
of boy who sat around waiting for foot spas to fall
from the sky, he had started planning months earlier.
First, he had tried to get a job but soon found that
giving jobs to boys his age was illegal, for reasons
Alfie could not understand. When the letter he had
written to the Prime Minister on the subject had
gone unanswered he had been forced to fall back on
his fallback plan, or 'Plan B' as he liked to call it.

Plan B was complicated. First Alfie had opened
an online bank account with the five pounds his
mum had given him for his own birthday. For the
next two weeks he spent every spare moment in the
library studying *The Financial Times*, seven or eight
hideously dull books about the stock market, and
magazines such as *Investment Today*. By the time he
understood words like 'liquidity' and 'leverage' he
felt ready for the third and final stage of his scheme.

Using the library's computer he had transferred the five pounds from his bank account and started buying stocks and shares; watching carefully as rows of brain-manglingly complex numbers rose and fell on the screen.

His efforts had paid off. Five pounds had become six pounds and eighty-seven pence, which had become eight pounds thirty. For most of the summer holiday, Alfie sat in the library buying and selling more shares while his mum was at work. Over six weeks, he had triumphed. His fiver turned into one hundred pounds.

And then the stock market had slowed.

It hadn't been a catastrophic crash; more of a mild prang, but it meant that Alfie's hundred quid just sat there, blinking on the computer screen and stubbornly refusing to become one hundred and forty-nine pounds and ninety-nine pence. With just one day until his mum's birthday, his plans lay in tatters. The foot spa seemed an impossible dream.

He needed a new plan: a Plan C. Stuffing the book and magazine in his backpack, he flicked open yesterday's copy of *City News*, which his mum had left on the kitchen table. Brain whizzing, he leafed through the pages without really seeing them. For a second he considered walking into Foot Spa World and stuffing the Sole Sensation 6000 up his jumper but quickly tossed the thought aside with the contempt it deserved. He gritted his teeth. His mum *was* going to wake up on her birthday to find a nicely wrapped Sole Sensation 6000 at the end of her bed. *Whatever it took . . .*

Alfie blinked. His eyes focused on the newspaper and opened wide. He gulped a deep breath.

Without thinking, he had turned the newspaper's pages to the classified section of small adverts. In the middle of the page Plan C stared back at him. Carefully, he drew a ring around it as his mum opened her bedroom door.

'OK then, son, I'm off. See you in twelve to fourteen hours,' she said.

Hurriedly, Alfie rustled the newspaper closed. 'OK,' he said, 'have fun at work.' As soon as the words left his mouth, he knew they were stupid. Gutting fish for twelve to fourteen hours is almost never fun.

If she thought it was a stupid thing to say, his mother didn't mention it. Instead, she dropped a kiss on his forehead. 'Have fun yourself,' she replied. 'Tonight my goat in a bonnet is going to crush your leg-warmer goat.'

'In your dreams,' Alfie shouted as the door closed.

Taking a deep breath, he opened the newspaper again, and checked the advert. It was still there. He glanced at the clock. It was 7.30 a.m. If he moved fast he would be on time. Forcing down the urge to run, he waited a few minutes for his mum to get down the stairs to the street, then walked three steps to his bedroom to collect his coat, followed by six steps to the front door. The flat really was *that* tiny.

CLASSIFIEDS

FRIDGE MAGNET. Large magnet shaped like a fridge. Saucepans, cutlery, and all my teeth fillings stuck to it: £325. Call 85641

STANLEY'S ANKLES. Fed up with looking at skinny ankles? Our motto is 'Feast your eyes on them lovely plump ankles.' Call 15687 and ask for Stanley.

HELP NEEDED due to bad back. Mostly carrying and lifting. £49.99 paid in cash for one day's work. Would suit a young person with a taste for adventure and no back problems. Apply in person, 8.30 a.m. sharp tomorrow. 4, Wigless Square.

CLOWN SHOES. Four feet long. Red leather. Haunted by the ghost of Jimmu, first emperor of Japan, hence bargain price: £750 the pair. Call 65914

SLUGS! SLUGS! SLUGS! £60 each. Call 37856. No timewasters.

BATHWATER. Hardly used. £10. Call 14685

CHAPTER TWO
THE STRANGE PROFESSOR

Wigless Square was an odd kind of place, Alfie thought. To get there he had pushed and jostled through busy streets heaving with people and buses and taxis and shops blaring music, or neat squares packed with posh houses and expensive cars. Wigless Square was nothing like the rest of the city though. Buildings and houses of every possible age and style crowded around a small, overgrown garden in its centre. Most had been boarded up or had broken windows. Here and there were a few signs of life: an ancient and battered Rolls-Royce that had been parked halfway up the pavement; a takeaway restaurant called the Happy Dragon that looked anything but happy; a door with peeling paint, open and leading into a gloomy hallway. Mostly though, the square looked deserted, and was silent apart from the distant traffic rumble. In the middle of the garden stood a statue of a bald man spattered with pigeon droppings. Alfie checked the address in the newspaper, and looked up again at Number Four. Putting his head to one side, he tried to find a single straight line in the building, and failed. Squeezed between an old mansion and a decaying office block like an elderly drunk propped up between two younger friends, the old house leant heavily on its neighbours. The thatched roof was buckled; its beams twisted and black with age. Alfie could see patches in the wall where ancient mud had fallen away. Beneath, the house looked as if had been woven together from twigs. A barrier of yellow tape had been put up along the pavement outside. Alfie ducked beneath it and peered at the notice pinned to the door.

HAZARDOUS BUILDING

By order of the council, Number Four, Wigless Square, has been found to be in a dangerous state, breaching rules 3589b and 5879c of the council code. Unless repairs are begun within fourteen days of this notice, the property will be demolished with no further warning.

Alfie checked the date. The notice had been put up thirteen days ago. He shrugged. It would be a shame to demolish such an interesting old house and under normal circumstances he would have written someone a letter about it. Today, he had other things on his mind. Pulling himself up to his full height and making sure his knees were both pointing in the same direction, he rapped on the door.

Nothing happened.

Alfie rapped again.

Faintly, through thick oak, he heard a scuffling. He rapped once more. After a few moments a voice on the other side of the door shouted, 'I'm not here.'

Alfie frowned at the door. He hadn't shoved

his way through the rush hour to be turned away without even getting an interview. 'Where are you then?' he shouted back.

'I'm . . . ah . . . I'm in Helsinki.'

Alfie considered his next move. He didn't want to ruin his chances of getting the job by calling his employer a liar before the door had even opened. Carefully, he replied, 'You're in Helsinki? The capital of Finland? *Really*?'

A pause. 'I might be,' the voice shot back eventually.

'How does that work then?' Alfie shouted. 'Only it sounds exactly like you're standing on the other side of this door.'

'I could be throwing my voice, like those people with the dummies. I've seen them do that. Ventriloquists! That's what they're called.'

'Throwing your voice from *Helsinki*? It's a thousand miles away.'

'One thousand, two hundred and eighty-three miles and a bit. That's measuring to Helsinki city centre, of course. If I was staying further out, perhaps in a nice bed and breakfast along the coast, then I wouldn't need to throw my voice quite so far . . .'

'Well, could you give me an interview, wherever you are?' shouted Alfie. 'I've come about the job, you see.'

'Well why didn't you say so? I thought you were from the council.' The door burst open.

'Gah,' said Alfie, stepping backwards. Framed in the doorway was a man with a huge moustache. So far, so good. The moustache was a bristling monstrosity but Alfie was prepared to live and let live. However, below the moustache, everything else was more than a little bit odd. Alfie definitely hadn't been expecting the billowing silk dressing gown, printed with flowers. The old man was also wearing a tight, old-fashioned ladies' corset and the sort of stained, grey, long underwear that old men love. On his feet were curly-toed, tasselled slippers. Hanging around his neck on a chain was a miniature gramophone, complete with trumpet attachment.

Stretching out a hand that was wearing a pink rubber glove, the old man said, 'Professor Pewsley Bowell-Mouvemont, at your service.'

He looked as barmy as a badger. Thinking back over the Helsinki conversation, Alfie decided he probably *was* as barmy as a badger. Nevertheless, Alfie needed a job and the old man seemed the sort of person who wouldn't care much whether it was legal or not. He took the Professor's hand and shook it. 'Alfie Fleet. Pleased to meet you,' he said, letting the Professor's glove go. 'Bowell-Mouvemont? That's an . . . um . . . interesting name.'

'It's French,' the Professor replied. 'Wonderful people, though it's a shame about their hats. *Berets* they call them. Look like cowpats I always think. Still, they do amazing things with cheese. I do like cheese, especially a nice slice of Cheddar. Or Stilton if you have any. What kind of cheese did you say you were selling, Rupert?'

Alfie took a deep breath before replying, then said, 'It's Alfie, and I don't have any cheese.'

'No cheese?' The Professor's voice sounded disappointed. 'What on Earth are you doing selling it from door-to-door then?'

'I came about the job,' Alfie replied.

'Ah yes, of course. The job, the job. Of course,

of course, of course. Forget my own . . . ummm . . .
thingy next,' replied the Professor. 'The job. Righty-
ho. So, we'll be off almost immediately and away for
three or four days so I wish I could offer more but I
only have forty-nine pounds ninety-nine pence. On
the bright side, we'll be finished later this afternoon.
Well, what are you waiting for? Come in, Rupert,
come on in.'

Alfie hopped from one foot to the other,
nervously. 'Look,' he said, 'I don't want to sound
rude but is this a *real* job? Only you seem a bit
gah—' The sentence was cut short when the
Professor reached out a hand, grabbed the front of
Alfie's jumper, and yanked him inside. The door
slammed.

'Hey, you can't do—' Alfie began. Once again, he
didn't finish the sentence.

'It's the man from the council,' the Professor
hissed, dropping to his knees and peering
through the letterbox. 'Across the square. I see
you, Wrenchpenny, with your hair gel and your
fashionable spectacles and your "unfit for human
habitation" . . .'

But Alfie barely heard him. Jaw hanging open, he spun in the middle of the house's entrance hall. Occasionally, another '*gah*' escaped his throat.

The place was . . . it was . . . Alfie searched for the right word and decided that 'amazing' would have to do, though amazing wasn't the half of it. Soft light streaming in through dirty, diamond-paned windows gleamed on old brass and red leather and what looked like the contents of a bizarre museum. *Several* bizarre museums, in fact. The place was stuffed to the brim with weirdness. A totem pole leant against the wall in one corner, carved with alien-looking creatures. Strange contraptions whirred and clicked around the floor. On the far side of the room stood a statue of a woman with pointed ears and hardly any clothes. There were skeletons that looked human but were smaller than Alfie's hand,

and the helmet of a suit of armour
that must have been made for a
giant. On the walls hung framed
black-and-white photographs—a
group of odd-looking people
sat outside a tent pitched in a
jungle made of tentacles; the
Professor with his arm round a
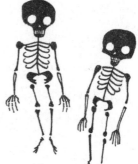
centaur; a signed photo of a man with two heads,
both of which were wearing sunglasses; an elderly
woman in a tweed skirt leaning on a sword next to
a long-haired man wearing leather
underpants. Elsewhere, globes of
planets that were very definitely
not Earth stood on heavy oak
tables. A peculiar hang-glider
made from skins hung from
the ceiling and everywhere
Alfie looked there were books.
Great leather-bound tomes sat
in stacks alongside heaps of
yellowed scrolls.

There was much, much more to look at but a loud banging interrupted Alfie's gawping. It was followed by a voice yelling, 'Open up. I know you're in there. Come on. If you can't afford to fix the place up you've got to leave.'

Turning, Alfie saw the Professor's face turn red with anger. 'I'm not leaving, Wrenchpenny,' he shouted through the letterbox.

'Come on, Professor,' Wrenchpenny continued in a wheedling voice. 'The house is dangerous. You've had your chance to repair it and the council's patience has run out. It has to be demolished, starting tomorrow. But I've found a lovely place for you to stay. Three meals a day, a nurse to help you on and off the toilet, a television in the common room . . . What do you say?'

'I say you're a disgusting thief,' the Professor bellowed. 'Now get lost!'

From the other side of the door, the man from the council said, 'I've tried being nice you silly old fool but you can't stop this place being torn down.'

'I've got another day,' shouted the Professor.

'Heh,' Wrenchpenny chuckled. 'It'll cost at least

half a million to repair. Where are you going to find that kind of money by tomorrow? Face it, Prof, you've got to go.'

Deciding the Professor's money problems were none of his business, Alfie tried not to listen. Instead, he shuffled from foot to foot and stared at the wall where a selection of maps had been pinned. Like the globes, they showed places that Alfie had never seen in any geography lesson. Some were faded, drawn on to yellow parchment. The newest, while a little battered, looked as though the ink was barely dry.

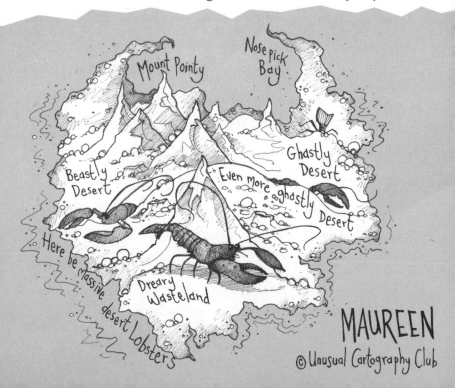

Mount Pointy

Nose pick Bay

Ghastly Desert

Beastly Desert

Even more ghastly Desert

Here be massive desert Lobsters

Dreary Wasteland

MAUREEN
© Unusual Cartography Club

'I'll be back this afternoon,' Wrenchpenny threatened through the door. 'If you haven't raised the money by then I'm getting the police to drag you out.'

'We'll just see about that, you repulsive toad,' the Professor thundered back. 'You can try evicting a Bowell-Mouvemont but you can expect a long, hard struggle, I promise you that.'

Alfie turned to watch the Professor glaring through the letterbox as the man from the council retreated. Pretending not to notice the tear that rolled down the old man's face, he said, 'Um, is this a bad time? I could come back later.'

'Time is something we cannot afford to waste,' said the Professor, struggling to his feet with a hand on his creaking back. 'We have a number of places to visit. Let's get Betsy loaded up and we'll be off. Follow me.'

'Er . . . I have a few questions first, if you don't mind?' Alfie said as the Professor strode away.

The Professor stopped. Turning, he said, 'Fire away.'

'Thanks, well I have quite a few questions

actually, but let's start with three.'

'Let's have 'em.'

'First,' said Alfie. 'Will you be getting dressed? Properly dressed, I mean?'

The Professor looked down at his own clothing. 'Goodness,' he squawked in surprise.

'Second,' Alfie continued, pointing at the map. 'Why have you drawn a map of a world called Maureen?'

'Ah, I just got back from Maureen. Named the planet after a girl I loved and lost as a young man,' said the Professor, tugging on his moustache. 'That's how I injured my back. Escaping. I was being chased across the desert by giant lobsters. Lucky I had Betsy, really.'

'I see,' said Alfie, who didn't see at all. Deciding to move on, he spread his arms to indicate the collection of curious souvenirs, and said, 'Third: what *is* this place?'

'Ah,' said the Professor, letting his baggy old eyes roam around the room. His face lit up with pride. 'This, Rupert, is the headquarters of the Unusual Cartography Club. Welcome.'

CHAPTER THREE
SMALLHENGE

Alfie stared at the front door while the Professor disappeared upstairs to get changed. Wrenchpenny had gone away and Alfie wondered if he should follow his example. Nothing the Professor had said made the slightest bit of sense. Questions fizzed in Alfie's head like a lemonade Jacuzzi. How could they be away for three or four days but finished that afternoon? Where did the Professor plan on taking him? Who was Betsy? What *exactly* was Alfie's job description? What on Earth was the Unusual Cartography Club? Cartography was the art of making maps—Alfie knew that much— but what was *unusual* cartography? Humans had explored every nook and cranny of planet Earth but the Professor had said he'd made a map of another planet. A planet called Maureen. That couldn't be possible. Clearly, Alfie thought to himself, he was dealing with a very odd man.

Creeping out was the sensible thing to do. Alfie wouldn't be able to afford the Sole Sensation 6000 but his mum might be just as happy with the Sweet Feet 2000, although it had neither Soothejet Technology nor Toe-Polishers.

On the other hand, Alfie was the kind of boy who enjoyed books about the weird and wonderful, and he was standing in the entrance hall of a house that fitted that description perfectly. Lifting his gaze from the door, he looked around at shrunken heads; the metal hand in a glass case; a football-sized airship that was slowly circling the room. He *could* creep out, but it would mean his curiosity would never be satisfied.

'Ready to go, Rupert?'

Alfie looked up to see the Professor clomping down the staircase. The old man had changed into a dark-green, old-fashioned and battered-looking velvet suit, which had a long, long coat with sleeves the old man could have hidden a badger in. Underneath he wore a pink, frilly shirt. His boots were black—an improvement on the slippers, Alfie thought—but still had curly toes. The miniature gramophone still hung around his neck. In one hand was a clipboard, with a pencil dangling from a length of string. On his head was an open-faced motorcycle helmet with goggles. If anything the outfit made him look even more peculiar than the silk dressing gown and corset.

'Yes,' Alfie nodded. 'Yes, I'm ready.'

'Marvellous,' said the Professor. Turning on his heel, he marched away. Looking back over his shoulder, he barked, 'Come along then. First stop: Outlandish.'

'Hang on,' said Alfie hurrying out of the entrance hall and along a corridor after the Professor. 'Don't you want to interview me first? I might be completely unsuitable for the job.'

The Professor stopped and peered back at Alfie. 'Good point, well made. Got to do these things properly, I suppose. Name: Rupert. Check. Can you lift things, Rupert?'

Alfie nodded.

'Lifting things. Check. Well I'm delighted to tell you that you've got the job. Knew you'd pass the interview. I was rooting for you all the way. Come along, nearly there.' Once more, the Professor strode off down the corridor, turned right, opened a door, and led Alfie down a long, stone staircase into a cavern.

Which was a surprise. In Alfie's experience not many houses in the city had actual caverns underneath them. It was made of brick and didn't have any stalactites or stalagmites, so Alfie momentarily thought about calling it a 'cellar' but cellars weren't usually lit by flaming torches and—as far as Alfie knew—cellars weren't often big enough to contain massive stone circles. It was definitely a cavern, he decided. A cavern with a stone circle in it. 'Gah,' said Alfie again. Then, feeling like he needed a new way to express strong surprise, he added 'Wah?'

'Impressive, isn't it?' said the Professor.

'Um . . . yes . . . "impressive" . . . that's exactly the word I was thinking of,' Alfie said, though the word he had really been thinking of was 'impossible'.

Against the cavern walls were overflowing chests
and stacks of drawers. An old and rusty moped
stood propped up on its stand. Alfie barely glanced at
any of those things. He was too busy goggling at the
stone circle.

'The Club used to use Stonehenge,' the Professor
continued. 'But that was a long time ago. Problem

was you had to move the stones around by hand,
and that's a bother. Plus, the place was always
crowded with people in robes—worshipping the
sun, or something. They get in the way, you see, and
complain like anything when you start shifting the
place around. Turned out it was easier just to build
our own stone circle. This is only half the size but it's

on a rotating platform, so much easier to operate. Very clever.'

'Mmmm,' Alfie agreed. 'Very clever. But . . . um . . . *why*?'

'Why what?'

'Why have you got a rotating stone circle in a cavern below your house?'

'What *do* they teach young people in school these days?' the Professor puffed. 'We use it for travel purposes, *obviously*. I did mention this is the Unusual Cartography Club, didn't I? Are you by any chance a little bit slow, Rupert? Only I didn't think to ask during the interview and—'

'Alfie,' Alfie interrupted. Feeling like he was in a dream he crossed the stone floor. 'Travel,' he repeated, gazing up at the towering stones. They didn't look as if they'd go very far. He took a step forward and put a hand on one. The stone was definitely stone. The half-size Stonehenge wasn't some kind of complicated prank made from polystyrene.

'Travel,' the Professor confirmed. 'We line the circle up to the correct coordinates and . . . No.

Wait. It's activated. Don't walk through the—'

The Professor's voice cut off abruptly as Alfie stepped into a silence so deep he could hear himself blink, and a darkness that stretched out for infinity in every direction. For half a heartbeat he felt like he was floating in an endless and empty universe.

And then he was somewhere else.

Alfie blinked again, several times. Every time he opened his eyes he hoped that the sight before them would change.

It didn't.

Alfie tried one last blink. It still didn't work, so he looked around instead. The view was utterly alien and totally mind-melting. Somehow, with one step between two pillars of the stone circle, he had been transported away from the cavern below Number Four, Wigless Square. Above him the sky spun with strange galaxies. The ground beneath his feet was black, polished metal. As if all that wasn't weird enough, stretching away from him in every direction were rows and rows and rows of gigantic glass jars; each filled with glowing pink liquid; each containing an enormous, floating brain.

'Sheesh,' Alfie whispered to himself. He peered at the closest jar. The number 2,698,787,238,969 had been etched into the glass.

The Professor stepped out of nowhere to stand beside him.

2,698,787,238,9

'Ah,' he said. 'Brains-in-Jars World. Every circle resets to Brains-in-Jars World after a while. No one knows why.'

'Ooooo-*kay*,' Alfie said, slowly. 'So I'm either standing on a different world or I've gone bonkers. Do I look like I've gone bonkers?'

'Not at all,' said the Professor, giving him a friendly pat on the shoulder. 'It can affect you like that the first time though, Brains-in-Jars World. I mean, you can't help wondering what they're all doing in there, eh?'

'What *are* they all doing in there?' asked Alfie.

'Good question, to which the answer is "who knows?" Samantha Sibilant—a brilliant but rather peculiar woman who was President of the UCC when I was a lad—had a theory that the brains dream the universe into being. Without them nothing would exist, she thought.'

'And what do *you* think?' Alfie asked.

'I think old Samantha was one of those mad scientists you hear about,' said the Professor, giving Alfie a nudge with a bony elbow. 'I think it's probably just a lot of brains in jars. One of those things. It's pretty big, the universe, and you see all sorts when you're out and about. A few of us mounted an expedition once though, to see if we could disprove her theory.'

Alfie couldn't help but be curious. 'How would you do that?' he asked.

'We thought we'd turn the brains off and back on again,' said the Professor, tugging on his moustache. 'See what happened.'

'You did *what*?'

'Couldn't find the off-switch though,' the Professor continued.

'But what if you *had* found it? What if she'd been *right*?' Alfie gasped. 'What if you'd destroyed the entire universe at the flick of a switch?'

The Professor shrugged. 'That would have left us looking a bit silly, I suppose,' he said. 'But we're not getting anything done, standing here chattering like clams. Brains-in-Jars World is of no real interest. No cartography, see? No continents or mountains or rivers. Nothing. Whole planet's like this. Billions and billions of brains in jars and you know what they say—seen one giant brain in a jar and you've seen them all. Come along then. I'm not paying you to stand around gawping. Outlandish awaits.'

'You're absolutely *certain* I'm not bonkers?' Alfie asked.

'Of course, of course, of course,' Professor Bowell-Mouvemont chuckled. 'You're no more bonkers than I am.'

Alfie was not reassured. On the Scale of Nuttiness, the Professor scored very highly, but Alfie decided he had two choices. He could either panic because somewhere between his mum's flat and Wigless Square he had lost his mind, *or* he could choose to believe that he really was standing on an alien planet with a man who—if the creaking noises when he moved were any clue—was *still* wearing a corset.

The second option seemed more fun. '*Wow*,' he said, cheerfully. 'So, the stone circle acts as a portal to other worlds, does it? That's pretty cool. How *many* other worlds?'

The Professor patted his shoulder again. 'Why, *all* of them,' he chuckled.

CHAPTER FOUR
THE PERKS AND BENEFITS OF INTERGALACTIC TRAVEL

Back in the cavern beneath Number Four, Wigless Square, the Professor waved his pencil towards the far corner. 'Next, two spare cans of petrol. In the cupboard over there.'

Alfie fetched the sloshing cans and carefully tied them to the back of the moped, which the Professor had named 'Betsy'. The rusty old scooter was already piled high. Sweating a little, he watched the Professor from the corner of his eye. The old man was perched on a stool like a scrawny walrus in a crash helmet, poring over an enormous, leather-bound book, mumbling to himself, and making occasional notes. Alfie didn't like to interrupt him but curiosity prodded at him until he blurted a question: 'Why do we need all this stuff if we're going to be back later this afternoon?'

- Tea-making equipment ✓
- Tents x 2 ✓
- Sleeping bags x 2 ✓
- Moustache-grooming kit ✓
- Folding table, chairs, tablecloth, vase, and candlesticks ✓
- Sandwiches ✓
- Surveying equipment and whatnot ✓
- General Stuff, inc. things ✓
- Professor Pewsley Bowell-Mouvemont ✓
- Shoe polish, iron, ironing board, clothes brush ✓
- MAP! ✓
- Spare petrol—two cans

The Professor looked up. 'Later this afternoon in three or four days. I did say, didn't I?'

'Yes, but it didn't make any sense then either.'

'Hmm, how to explain?' The Professor fiddled with his moustache. 'Imagine if I threw a cabbage at you while you were running away. It would hit you much less hard than if you were running towards me, wouldn't it? Do you see what I'm getting at?'

'You're saying that . . .'

'I can see the cabbage thingy isn't really working,' the Professor interrupted. 'Putting cabbages aside, although I do like a bit of boiled cabbage. My old mam used to make it just . . .'

'Putting cabbages aside,' Alfie prompted.

'Oh yes. So, as I was saying: in a nutshell, not to put too fine a point on it, when push comes to shove . . . where was I?'

Alfie sighed. 'I think you were trying to explain that time moves more slowly where we're going,' he said.

'Oh yes. So you see, young Rupert, where we're going, time moves much more *slooowly*. Do you understand now?'

'It's like Albert Einstein,' Alfie nodded.

'Moves slowly, does he? Senior citizen, I'll bet. Not so light on his feet at his time of life, eh?'

'No, he was a scientist who said that time slows down the closer you get to the speed of light . . .' Seeing the baffled look on the Professor's face, Alfie continued, 'It doesn't matter.'

'So,' the Professor hurried on. 'We'll spend a day on Outlandish, which will take about half an hour of Earth time. Then a planet called Nerwong Nerwong Plinky-Plonk, then Earwax, before a couple of final checks on a world called Earwax II. To be honest, I was running out of new names when I discovered that one. If my calculations are correct, which they sometimes are, we'll be finished by late afternoon.'

'Hmm,' said Alfie. 'If time moves more slowly where we're going then I suppose that means you're paying me about five pounds an hour looking at it one way. Or about twenty pence an hour if you come at it in the opposite direction.'

The Professor blushed. 'Ah, yes. The budget is a little tight I'm afraid but there are perks and benefits, too,' he said.

'Perks and benefits?'

'Ah, well, you'll be an important part of the team, representing your country in far-off lands,' said the Professor. 'Plus, free travel, all the tea you can drink and . . . and . . .'

'It's all right,' said Alfie. 'I'm choosing to think that you're paying me five pounds an hour. And you're throwing in an extra three or four days of the school holiday, too. That's the petrol done, by the way. What's next?'

Brightening, the Professor picked his clipboard off the top of a chest, peered at it, and made a tick. 'That's the lot. Well done. I can see I made the right choice in hiring you. And look here, I've picked out the route across Outlandish we'll be taking.'

Alfie peered over the Professor's shoulder. As previous chapters have shown, he was—when all was said and done—a geeky kid, and his heart skipped at the sight before his eyes. Across the Professor's knees spread a map just like the maps he often saw in the opening pages of the books he loved. Books with names like *Darkheart Ravensword* or *Fist of the Beast King*. Unfamiliar mountain ranges and rivers snaked across an extraordinary continent. Galleons and sea monsters frolicked in the circling ocean. Printed in tiny letters next to castle symbols were places with exotic names like Gibbett Creaking and Fullgrave and Witch's Grim. To the north, the landscape stretched out into a landscape of snow and ice. Further south, a vast forest—labelled Hinderwood—cut the continent in two. The southern part of Outlandish looked more thickly populated. Places with names like Rogue's Shack and Disaster-on-Sea clung to the craggy coastline. Everywhere Alfie's eyes roamed across the page were hints of wilderness and wonder: a Griffen Isle, a Synistere Mountain, and a Wizard Home; a Valley of Lost Souls, and a Lake Trousers.

Head spinning for the third or fourth time that day—he had lost count—Alfie said, 'Wowzers,' quietly.

'This is the old edition of the Unusual Cartography Club's *Cosmic Atlas*,' Professor Bowell-Mouvemont said. He flicked through the pages.

Unusual worlds appeared before Alfie's eyes and disappeared again. 'Printed in 1802. Since then the club has been working on a new and updated edition with thirty-six worlds added. I mapped twelve myself. It's almost ready to go to the printers. You and I will just be double-checking the last few facts and figures.'

Alfie stared at him. 'You're going to publish it?' he gasped. 'But a genuine atlas of other worlds will be an instant bestseller! You'll make a fortune! You'll be able to pay to have the house repaired . . .'

'Ah, no, sadly not,' the Professor interrupted. 'There's just enough money left to have one copy printed, and that's for me. No one is interested in unusual cartography these days. It's . . . well . . . it's all technowloggy, isn't it? And celebritnies. And social mediums—whatever *they* are. No, I'm afraid the Unusual Cartography Club is broke. Like all the other clubs and societies around Wigless Square, it's going extinct.' He shrugged, wistful sadness in his old, red-rimmed eyes. 'Still, mustn't grumble, eh? I shall probably take up a hobby. Cucumbers, I thought.'

Alfie gazed down at the old book. Something so astounding, so gobsmackingly amazing, so . . . *unusual*, couldn't be allowed to come to an end. 'But that's not right,' he said. 'I'll write letters. I have the Prime Minister's address and . . . and . . . hang on. If this is a club, where are the other members? What are *they* doing about it?'

'All gone,' said the Professor. 'Dead, or they got lost or stranded on other planets or wandered off in worlds they liked better. It's just me now. So, you see, even if the Unusual Cartography Club could be saved there's no one to save it *for*. Oh, I'll put up a fight but eventually Wrenchpenny will have me dragged out of here with a few books and souvenirs and the place will be knocked down. Mustn't grumble, eh? All good things come to an end, Rupert. Even cucumbers.'

'But . . . but . . .' Alfie began.

'No point crying over what might have been,' said the Professor, wiping a tear from the corner of one eye. 'Come on. Time's a-wasting. Let's be off, eh? Strange worlds and new civilizations to seek out. These are the voyages of Professor Pewsley

Bowell-Mouvemont and Rupert . . . ah, I didn't catch your surname, Rupert.'

'Alfie,' said Alfie. 'Alfie Fleet.'

'Rupert Alfiealfiefleet,' said Professor Bowell-Mouvemont. 'Strange name. Norwegian is it?' Without waiting for a reply, he turned away and handed Alfie a crash helmet. 'You'll be needing this. And one of these, too,' he added, opening a drawer stuffed full of small gramophones on chains, like the one around his own neck.

CHAPTER FIVE

THE BOY EFFECT

The helmet was too big. Alfie strapped it on as best
he could while eyeing the gramophone necklace
dangling from the Professor's fingers. 'Do I have
to wear that?' he asked. 'Only it's not very stylish, is
it?'

The Professor looked Alfie up and down,
eyeing the sole flopping off one of his trainers, the
patched trousers that were a size too small, and the
unravelling wool at the cuffs of his faded pullover.
Raising an eyebrow, he cleared his throat and said,
'It's not supposed to be *stylish*.'

'What *is* it supposed to be then?'

'It's a translating gizmo, doodah, thingy,' said

the Professor. 'You twiddle the little handle here to wind the mechanism up and the box changes any language into English. Or vice versa. Mostly. Little tip: don't bother trying to translate anything that, say, a giant lobster might be trying to tell you. It just comes out as *squee squee squee*. Probably giant lobsters just aren't very good at making conversation.'

'But that's impossible . . .' Alfie began, and stopped. Impossible seemed to be having a day off. 'How does it work?' he asked instead.

'Like I said, you just twiddle the little handle and . . .'

'No, I mean how does it *work*?' Alfie interrupted. Taking the device from the Professor's hand, he turned it this way and that. Peering at it closely, he added, 'Is there a chip in it?'

The Professor shrugged. 'Could be a chip in it, though it would've gone cold by now. You'd have to ask Madelaine Tusk—she invented it. In 1787. Marvellous woman. She also came up with the rotation device for the stone circle and a wig that unfolded into a tent. You'd need to hold a seance though; she passed away a few years ago.' His voice broke into a panicked squeal as he continued, 'No. No, don't take it apart, Rupert. They tend to explode if you mess around with them and lifting and carrying is much harder with no fingers. Well, I say no fingers, but it'd probably take out the house, too, and the rest of the square. Plus surrounding areas. Half the city, I should think.'

Alfie stopped trying the prise the top off the tiny gramophone and hung it around his neck, carefully. '1787?' he said. 'How long has the club been around?'

'Now, now,' replied the Professor, waggling a finger in Alfie's face. 'While no one enjoys nosing into other people's business more than Professor Pewsley Bowell-Mouvemont, we do have those facts and figures to check. If you wouldn't mind seeing to Betsy, I'll spin the circle.'

Time for a quick interruption. Readers may be wondering the same thing as Alfie, and the answer to his question is that the Unusual Cartography Club has been around for about ten thousand years. Intergalactic historians say that it is the seventy-ninth oldest club in the universe. The oldest is—of course—the legendary Spanksy Book Club of planet Spanksy, which was formed soon after the universe began at a time when the only life on Spanksy was three bacteria living in a warm puddle. Oddly, the club existed for almost three billion years before anyone got round to inventing books.

Alfie had a bunch more questions, but he reminded himself that the old man was his new boss and bit his tongue—his own tongue, not the Professor's, because that would have been weird and is the sort of thing that gets people sacked. Returning to the moped, Alfie tightened a strap here and tugged a rope there. When he was certain the baggage wasn't going to fall off as soon as they started moving, he turned to watch the Professor. The old man was pushing hundreds of tonnes of standing stones into position as if the circle was as light as belly-button fluff. Below the platform, rollers purred and ratchets clicked. Every so often, the Professor consulted *The Cosmic Atlas* and made tiny adjustments, lining the circle up, just so, with markings on a copper ring set into the floor. Finally, he seemed satisfied. Tightening the strap of his helmet and pulling his goggles over his eyes, he crossed the stone floor, barking, 'All aboard for Outlandish. The Outlandish Express is now leaving Platform One.'

Obediently, Alfie settled his backside on the moped's seat. 'Make yourself useful and hold this,' said the Professor, thrusting *The Cosmic Atlas* into Alfie's hands before taking his own place and stamping down on the kick-starter. 'Squidge up behind,' he yelled above Betsy's coughing engine.

Alfie shuffled backwards, pressing back into the swaying tower of bags and equipment. The Professor pulled on the handlebars. Straining beneath the weight of two riders, the moped chugged twice around the stone circle. Clinging to the Professor's back, Alfie peered over his shoulder. The speedometer reached ten, then twelve, then fifteen miles an hour. 'Hold on tight,' the Professor shouted, yanking the handlebars once more and twisting the accelerator. 'Coming through. Toot toot.'

The needle trembled towards seventeen miles an hour as Betsy bounced up a ramp. Alfie heard a sound like 'Wheeeeeee' as she shot between the two largest stones. Once again, the boggling immensity of the universe unfolded around him.

Then, once again, he was somewhere else.

'Wheeeeee . . .' Realizing his own voice was making the 'whee' sound, and that it sounded silly, Alfie clamped his mouth shut.

The Professor slammed on the brakes. 'We have landed in Outlandish a few minutes behind schedule because certain young people kept asking questions,' he said. 'Local time is somewhere around mid-morning, I'd say.'

Almost blinded by the sudden daylight, Alfie rubbed his eyes and took a deep breath. He immediately felt giddy. After a lifetime in a polluted city the sharp, fresh air made his lungs burn and his brain fizz. Dazed, he clambered off the moped and looked around, open-mouthed, at a new world.

'Welcome to Outlandish,' said the Professor. 'If the locals haven't changed the names we are at a circle called 'Stoneygate'—very imaginative—on the great meadow of Summersniff, and those are the Hambanjo Mountains. We'll stop here for a while so I can take a few measurements. Good time to get the kettle on, eh Rupert? *Rupert?*'

Alfie didn't hear him. He was far too busy spinning on the spot, trying to take in the scenery. For the first time in his life he could see all the way to the horizon without grime-covered buildings blocking the view. Behind him was a stone circle so ancient and rickety that it looked like part of the landscape. On one side, the land flowed down to a lake in a meadow of grass and wild flowers. On the other it rose steeply into the sharp peaks of grey mountains. Rather than the grinding gears of buses and police sirens and people shouting, he could hear the tweeting of birds and the sleepy buzz of bees.

Alfie shook his head, trying to clear it. Since walking through the door of Number Four, Wigless Square, part of his brain hadn't trusted what it was seeing. The cavern and the stone circle and Brains-in-Jars World had all been too weird to really, *really*, deep-down, believe. But Outlandish wasn't like that. It was *completely* believable, and in its own way it was even weirder. The air was too zingy. The landscape was too wide. The sky was too blue. Suddenly, the fact that he was a bazillion miles from his home and his mum hit Alfie like a sock with a brick in it. It wasn't possible, he told himself. No human had ever travelled further than the moon. Scientists with their fancy space-telescopes and humming computers hadn't found a single world in the entire universe that could support human life. Yet he was standing on one, and it was one of *many* according to the Professor. The thought staggered him. He stumbled backwards. Tripping over his own feet, he reached out to steady himself on one of the pillars of the stone circle behind him.

Beneath his hand, it shifted.

Alfie spun round in time to see the great stone tip and fall. The word 'Meep,' escaped his lips.

'Yipes,' squawked the Professor as the rock groaned and fell into its neighbour. The second rock, too, groaned and fell, smashing into the next stone along, which—once again—groaned and fell.

Soon, all the rocks were at it, groaning and falling as if they'd been waiting for years to show off what they could do in the groaning and falling department. Alfie stepped back, staring in horror as the stone circle went down like the biggest set of dominos in creation.

To take another moment out of the story it's worth mentioning that disasters like this tend to happen around boys of Alfie's age. This is why it is illegal to give them jobs. They destroy pretty much everything they come in contact with. If the Professor had been a parent he would have known that this was exactly the right moment to yell, 'This is why we can't have nice things!' As it was, he just stood and stared, open-mouthed, as the route back to Earth collapsed.

Eventually, the crashing roar of a hundred tumbling rocks echoed away.

Silence fell, stretching out to every horizon.

More silence followed.

Then some more.

Someone had to say something. Alfie peered through the dust at the jumble of wrecked and broken stones. 'Will it still work?' he asked in a squeaky voice.

The Professor stepped over to stand beside him. Brushing stone dust from the velvet shoulder of his suit he tapped the closest stone with the toe of his boot and replied, quietly, 'Shouldn't think so. Looks a little bit out of order to me.'

'Can we fix it?'

'Hmm, good question, to which the answer is "not unless you're good at weaving daisies into, say, a full-size, working crane".'

'So we're stuck here then?'

'Mmm,' said the Professor, giving his moustache a tug.

'Oops,' squeaked Alfie. Panic gripped him. He squeaked again.

'Steady, Rupert,' the Professor replied, patting Alfie's shoulder. 'Always look on the bright side, I say. It could be worse. At least we have sandwiches.'

'Yes,' said Alfie, fighting back tears at the thought of never seeing his mum again. Between clenched teeth, he said, 'At times like this a sandwich is such a great comfort.'

'That's the spirit,' chuckled the Professor. 'Nothing like a sandwich when you're upset. If you dig them out of the luggage I'll set the table.'

'Shall I get sandwiches for them, too?' said Alfie, pointing to a tall, bearded man with grizzled hair who was striding towards them. He was draped in robes and had a set of antlers strapped to his head. Behind him were dozens of men, women, and children, their faces painted, dressed in animal skins, and armed with bows and arrows. 'Only they look a bit upset, as well.'

CHAPTER SIX

SKINGRATH'S CHEESED-OFF CHILDREN

'Oomm baff ta gorhahaha Skingrath,' raged the antler-headed leader of the warrior band, pointing a shaking finger at the heap of fallen stones. 'Wollooom pan tatarta Skingrath taramasalata.'

The Professor twiddled the handle on the side of his gramophone necklace. 'Sorry, didn't catch that,' he said. 'Say again.'

Trembling with rage, the antler-man spoke again. This time, to Alfie's amazement, the words were sucked up by the gramophone and spat out from the tiny trumpet in perfect English. 'You have destroyed the shrine of the great god Skingrath,' the man roared. 'Now, the Children of Skingrath will sacrifice your lives on the god's blood-soaked altar.'

Still twiddling, the Professor gave Alfie a wink. 'This happens all the time,' he said. 'People find an old stone circle and think some silly god put it there.'

To Alfie's horror, the words came out of the gramophone in perfect Outlandish. He watched as the antlered man's face turned from red to purple.

'Um . . . he's listening to you, and I don't think he's very happy,' Alfie whispered back.

In fact, antler-man, who Alfie decided must be some sort of priest, was trembling with anger. 'Seize them,' he hissed. 'Their sacrifice will please Skingrath.'

In less than a second, Alfie found himself at the centre of a circle of warriors. Hands grabbed his arms. The strings of drawn bows thrummed tightly. Alfie couldn't help noticing that although the arrows were made of wood and feathers, they looked horribly pointy. 'What now?' he croaked.

'Don't worry. I'll have this sorted out in a second,' said the Professor. Turning back to the priest, he said in a loud, slow voice, 'Now, look here, I'm not sure you understand the situation . . .'

Alfie gulped and squeezed his eyes closed. The expedition, which had started so excitingly, was going from awful to terrifying. As if the collapse of the route home wasn't bad enough, he was about to be sacrificed. He really, *really* didn't want to be sacrificed, but any moment now the Professor was going to tell the Children of Skingrath that the circle wasn't a shrine and that their god didn't exist. He had a feeling they'd take the news badly.

Instead, the Professor said, 'I *am* Skingrath, do you see?'

A gasp rippled through the Children of Skingrath. At the same time Alfie's eyes opened, hands released him. The crowd had fallen to its knees. Warriors stared up at the Professor, many with tears of joy in their eyes. Only the priest remained standing. He had folded his arms and was tapping a foot, glaring suspiciously. 'Speak then, fierce Skingrath,' he hissed. 'Tell us why you have destroyed your own shrine.' He nodded, as if to say 'Get out of that one'.

'Oh, that's easy,' the Professor continued. 'Since

you ask, I—Skingrath—am an angry god and I'm fed up with you people. You're getting this religion thing all wrong. Too many sacrifices. Not enough good works. I command that you be nice to people. Take the old folks on a day out now and then. As I've always said, a kind word is better than a meal of wasps.'

The Children of Skingrath pressed their foreheads to the ground. Moans of despair drifted across the meadow as they received a telling-off from their god.

Talking out of the corner of his mouth, the Professor added, 'Did that sound holy enough?'

Alfie couldn't have been more surprised if the Professor had announced he was an eel named Raymond. Unable to find a reply, he nodded.

'Good, good,' the Professor chuckled. Turning back to the Children of Skingrath, he continued, 'So, I say unto you that the poor shall inherit the thingumajig and the meek shall feast on apple crumble. Did I mention good works? I did, didn't I? So that's all right then. In my holy name, Amen. Well, you've been a lovely audience.

Thank you and goodbye.'

'But is it not written that Skingrath is a fearsome god?' the priest interrupted. 'With three heads, hair of fire, and great big tusks. He teaches us to make war upon our enemies.'

'Oh, for goodness' sake,' the Professor tutted. 'I'm sorry but you're starting to get on my nerves. Great big tusks indeed! The cheek of it. Now, if you'll excuse me, my . . . erm . . . angel . . . and I will be leaving on this . . . um, magic metal horse.'

Alfie felt an elbow dig into his ribs. Jolted into action, he began edging towards Betsy. 'All praise the great Skingrath!' he shouted.

'And his angel?' asked one of the warriors, raising his head from the ground. 'Should we praise him, too?'

Alfie felt himself blush. 'Really, there's no need,' he mumbled.

'Oh yes,' the Professor bellowed. 'All praise the angel Rupert, too.'

'It's Alfie, actually,' said Alfie in a small voice. He hadn't asked to be praised, but if people were going to insist then at least they could get his name right.

Unfortunately, no one was paying him any attention. Shouts of 'Hail, great Skingrath' and 'Hail, holy Rupert,' echoed in his ears as Alfie swung a leg over Betsy. The Professor scrambled into the saddle in front of him. 'Goodbye then,' the old man shouted, with a wave. 'Don't forget what I said about being nice to people, will you?'

The priest was still glaring, hatred in his eyes. As Betsy's engine spluttered into life, he screamed, '*Lies*! He called our god silly. I heard him say that. He is not Skingrath. He is Jael, the Deceiver. Skingrath's mighty fury shall fall upon him.'

Betsy lurched forwards, with Alfie staring wide-eyed at the scene he and the Professor were leaving behind. The priest raised his hands. Above his head dark clouds boiled from a clear sky. Lightning spat. Wind lashed Alfie's hair around his face. 'Kill them!' screamed the priest. 'Do not let them escape. Kill the false Skingrath, and his little angel, too.'

The first arrow bounced off Alfie's crash helmet at the same moment that the first fat raindrop slapped his face. A spear of lightning smashed into the ground, close by, leaving a smoking hole. Clinging to the Professor's back as Betsy gathered speed, bouncing and slipping across the wet meadow, Alfie yelled, 'He's doing magic. He's doing real-life *magic*!'

Hands gripping Betsy's handlebars, wringing every last drop of power from her straining engine, the Professor shouted back, 'I wouldn't be at all surprised. He did seem a bit cheesed off.'

Another arrow hit the baggage by Alfie's head. Something smashed. 'My second-best plates,' growled the Professor. 'The fiends! The tablecloth's going to be full of arrow holes, too, and I embroidered that myself. Took me *ages* to do all the pansies.' Lightning sizzled and flashed. Bobbing down in the saddle, Alfie risked another glance back. The priest stood before the ruined circle, magical power flaring from his raised fists. Around him, the warriors' bows twanged and twanged again, sending a hurricane of arrows after Alfie and the Professor.

Betsy hit a rock and skidded in mud. Holding

on to the Professor's back as if his life
depended on it—which it did—Alfie ducked
lower. He was surprised to find that although
he was close to wetting himself with terror he
was slightly less scared than he was annoyed.
The Professor had told him he'd be doing some
light lifting and carrying.

Being stranded and shot at and fried to a crisp by magical lightning had definitely *not* been in the job description. If it had been, Alfie told himself, he'd have asked for a lot more than forty-nine pounds and ninety-nine pence.

CHAPTER SEVEN

TEATIME ON OUTLANDISH

Betsy was not fast but she was slightly faster than
a bunch of people wearing scooped-out rabbits
for shoes, and she didn't need to stop to catch
her breath. As the moped bounced across the
grasslands, the Children of Skingrath fell further
and further behind. After a while, the magical storm
fizzled out, too. Rays of sunshine split the clouds.
Alfie's terror faded. Instead, a dark pit of worry
opened up in his stomach, fighting his full bladder
to see which could make him more uncomfortable.
The stone circle had collapsed. Time might be
moving more slowly back in London but if he and
the Professor couldn't find a way back to Earth his

mum would eventually get home from work and discover him gone. She'd try and find him, then panic, then call the police. And unless the police had a secret intergalactic missing persons squad they would fail to find him. Alfie would have simply vanished and his mum would never know what had happened to him.

It was an awful thought, but Alfie had to admit to himself that it wasn't his most immediate problem. With every jolt he was getting closer and closer to leaving a damp patch on Betsy's saddle. Tapping the Professor on the shoulder, he shouted, 'Can we stop now?'

★ ✶ ★

'That was unexpected,' he said ten minutes later, peering over the rim of a china cup and enjoying the sensation of a freshly emptied bladder. 'The Skingrath thing, I mean. Wasn't it a bit . . . er . . . *wrong* to tell those people you're a god?'

'Standard procedure,' said the Professor, swallowing the last crumb of a cheese sandwich. He slumped in his folding chair, puffed on his own cup to cool the hot tea, and set it down in its saucer. 'Saves unpleasantness. No one likes being told their holy place isn't all that holy. Funnily enough, I'm worshipped on at least fourteen worlds. They built a statue on Vavoom Six. Seventy metres tall. Didn't get the nose quite right though.'

'So who was Skingrath?' Alfie asked. 'The original Skingrath, I mean.'

'Probably just some alien creature who wandered into a stone circle somewhere else by mistake. That happens from time to time if you leave them open.' The Professor picked up his tea again and stared gloomily into the cup. Even his moustache drooped.

'Is everything OK?' Alfie asked.

A wince crossed the Professor's face. 'Not really,' he mumbled. 'Total disaster, eh? Probably missing your mum already. Might never see her again. My responsibility. Expedition leader and all that.'

'It wasn't your fault, Professor. *You* didn't get us stranded. *I* pushed the circle over, remember? Plus, you saved my life back there. They were going to sacrifice us. I should be thanking you.'

'Even so . . .' began the Professor.

Alfie interrupted. 'Besides,' he said, firmly. 'We *are* going to get home.'

The Professor gave Alfie a nod of approval. 'Good lad,' he murmured. 'Just one tiny little question, if you don't mind . . . *How*?'

'There wasn't a circle on Brains-in-Jars World. Can't you just open a way home without one?'

'Ah,' replied the Professor, swirling his teacup unhappily. 'No. You can't just create a portal out of thin air. You need a circle to *open* a portal. It's not absolutely necessary to have one at the other end—you can just mark the exit with a couple of flags if you want to. We call that an Explorer's Pathway. You can use it to get home so long as you know where the exit is, but it's dangerous. If someone steals your flags, or they get blown away, or you forget *exactly* where the exit of the Explorer's Pathway comes out you may not find it again before the circle back home resets to Brains-in-Jars World. They all do that eventually, remember? And if that happens, you're stuck.'

'So that's why people build circles, then?' Alfie

asked. 'If you get stranded you can always use it to make a new link home?'

'Or travel anywhere else you fancy, yes,' said the Professor. 'But now Stoneygate is broken, and the exit of our portal will have closed when it collapsed. The way home is gone. I'm afraid we're in a bit of a pickle, Rupert.'

Alfie frowned. 'What about magic?' he asked after a few seconds. 'The priest of Skingrath did magic. Therefore, magic exists on Outlandish and all we need to do is find a wizard or witch and get them to, you know . . .' He waggled his fingers.

'Ah,' replied the Professor, sipping tea. 'Seen a lot of places where the locals wave their hands about, conjuring and all that. Never met anyone who could send two people halfway across the universe with no idea where they were going. Bit like flicking a rubber band at a moving fly. Blindfolded. We need a circle really.'

Alfie wasn't about to be beaten so easily. 'Can we build one?' he asked.

The Professor nodded. 'Oh yes,' he said.

'Then we'll do that,' said Alfie.

'If you don't mind mining tonnes of stones, chiselling them into the right shape, setting them up properly, spending ages making sure they're in exactly the right position, and then moving them all a millimetre clockwise if our measurements are slightly wrong and we don't hit Earth.'

'I see,' said Alfie. 'What if there's another circle somewhere on Outlandish? At least we wouldn't have to build one.'

The Professor brightened. 'That would be a start,' he said. 'Then all we'd need to do is turn it to the right coordinates. It would be a big job but with the right equipment and a few dozen people helping we might manage it in only a month or two.'

'Do we *really* need to do all that though?' said Alfie. 'If all circles reset to Brains-in-Jars World couldn't we just go there and find the place where the Wigless Square circle comes out?'

The Professor leapt to his feet. 'By the rotating nuns of Mundogo,' he yelped. 'The boy's got it. Any circle will reset to Brains-in-Jars World and so will ours. So if we can get to Brains-in-Jars World it would be a simple case of finding . . . oh, no. Wait.'

'What?'

'Brains-in-Jars World is a colossal planet, and the thing about brains in jars is that they all look the same,' sighed the Professor. 'We'd never find the place where our circle comes out.'

'We could follow the numbers. It comes out slightly to the left of jar number 2,698,787,238,969,' said Alfie.

The Professor stared at him. 'That's quite a memory you have there, young Rupert,' he said after a while.

Alfie was already rummaging in the baggage. Pulling *The Cosmic Atlas* from where he'd wedged it between a tent and the Professor's moustache-grooming kit, he licked a finger and began flicking through pages. 'Thanks,' he said. 'Sometimes I even remember that my name is Alfie. Let's see if Outlandish has any more circles, shall we?'

CHAPTER EIGHT

UPDATING THE ATLAS

It didn't.

Alfie checked the map six times, running his finger from an outpost called Shivverhoom in the far north to the tropical southern island of Mu'umbra. Stoneygate was the only stone circle on Outlandish, or, at least, the only one marked in *The Cosmic Atlas*.

'Hmm . . . There *might* be another one though,' the Professor said, peering over Alfie's shoulder. 'The UCC was a bit hit-and-miss back when the last *Cosmic Atlas* was printed.'

'Not like the sleek, professional Unusual Cartography Club of today,' Alfie muttered.

'*Exactly*,' said the Professor. 'The old crew often

overlooked things when we were putting the last *Atlas* together. Davy Gitspew once missed an entire volcano, and he was standing on it at the time. He was, of course, sharply reminded of its existence when it blew him into the upper atmosphere. Poor Davy. He went up like a firework, you know. It was quite a sight—'

By now, Alfie had learnt that the Professor's trips down memory lane could go on for some time. Interrupting, he said, 'So, if there is another circle, how do we find it?'

Taking another moment out of the story, it is worth mentioning that in his hurry to find another circle, Alfie failed to spot the fact that the Professor had been part of the expeditions to draw up the last *Cosmic Atlas*, which, if you remember, was published in 1802. That was a shame because if he *had* spotted it Alfie might have asked the Professor how old he was. The answer would have surprised him, because the Professor was, at the same time, somewhere in his sixties and about two hundred and fifty. He had been born in 1758 but skipped the best part of two hundred Earth years by visiting worlds where time moved much faster. For instance, he'd missed half of the nineteenth century while enjoying a game of Tweak with the Transparent Hivequeen of Cha-Cha-Cha.

Back to the story. Alfie was asking the Professor how they might find another circle . . .

'Asking around might do the trick,' the Professor replied, jabbing a finger at a large symbol on the map. 'We'd be bound to find someone who knows their way around Outlandish in a city that size.'

'It's called "(Den of Thieves)",' said Alfie. 'Why is it in brackets?'

'Ah, that's just a note someone's scribbled in.' The Professor moved his finger. 'See, it's called "Verminium". Sounds like fun, doesn't it?'

'No,' said Alfie.

The Professor wasn't listening. 'And it's only a hundred miles or so from here. We can be there tomorrow if we get moving.' Slurping the last of his tea, he set the cup down with a clatter of china and jumped to his feet. 'So you'd better pack up the tea things, Rupert.'

After rinsing the plates, cups, and saucers in a

nearby stream, carefully folding the tablecloth, and tying the rest of the gear back on to Betsy's tower of baggage, Alfie climbed back on to the moped, feeling better. There was a plan for getting home. It wasn't the best plan ever, but it was better than no plan at all.

After another fifteen miles or so, the little moped hit a road. Alfie's mood lifted even further. The road was little more than a muddy streak through the wilderness but it meant he wasn't bouncing up and down and having his bum whacked by a hard leather seat *all* the time. There was a signpost, too, pointing towards somewhere or other. The gramophone translators didn't work with writing, but this cheered Alfie up even more. A signpost meant there were people on Outlandish who might not be bloodthirsty weirdos with antlers strapped to their heads. For the first time since arriving, he took a proper look around at the landscape. Once again he was struck by the beauty of this strange new world. It looked a lot like Earth, but Earth before factories and cars and cities and advertising billboards. Wondering where they were, he pulled

The Cosmic Atlas out, opened it, and rested it against the Professor's back. 'It looks like we're in the Midelysian region,' he shouted over the engine noise. 'You're right about the old crew missing things though. This road isn't marked.'

'There's a pencil in the left saddlebag,' the Professor shouted back. 'Be a good lad and make a note, would you?'

Alfie scrawled a crooked line in the place he thought the road should be and sucked the end of his pencil. The Professor had said that only one copy of the new *Cosmic Atlas* would ever be printed, but it might fall into the hands of another traveller one day. Perhaps that future traveller would be grateful to find Alfie's road. Perhaps, Alfie thought, they might also find other information useful. He began to write in jerky letters as Betsy bounced onward . . .

TRAVEL WARNING

The west of the Midelysian region is home to a tribe of people known as the Children of Skingrath. Believers in a three-headed, warlike god, these not-very-charming Outlandish folk are easily recognized by their warpaint and the fact that they will probably be pointing weapons at you, blasting you with magical lightning bolts, and/or tying you to their sacrificial altar with your own intestines. They are to be avoided.

It would be nice if the traveller had some idea of what to expect in the Midelysian region, as well, Alfie thought. The map didn't really capture its prettiness. Alfie jotted a few more notes, by which time the map was starting to look messy. Digging around in the saddlebag, he found a notebook and continued.

DISCOVERING . . . MIDELYSIA

With its superb scenery, dotted with
ruined castles, burial mounds, and ancient
stone bridges, Outlandish's Midelysian
region is the place to be for anyone who
enjoys getting away from it all in the
great outdoors. Hikers and mountain
bikers will find a landscape brimming with
treasures, including waterfalls, ponds, and
sparkling streams, all of which probably
offer great fishing, too!

Alfie filled several pages of his notebook with
jagged, spiky writing while Betsy bounced on across
the landscape. The shadows lengthened, the sun
dipped below distant mountain peaks, and two
moons appeared above the horizon like a pair of
great glowing eyes staring down on the planet. He
was wondering what other information might go
into *The Cosmic Atlas* when the Professor interrupted

his thoughts. 'Looks like darkness is closing in, Rupert,' the old man said. 'We should look for a place to camp. We only brought two sandwiches so we'll have to dig up some grubs and roots for dinner, I'm afraid.'

Alfie looked up. 'We could do that,' he shouted, 'or that place looks like it might be an inn. Maybe we could stay there.' Leaning forward, he pointed over the Professor's shoulder to a building ahead, half-hidden by trees. Candlelight glowed in small windows. Smoke billowed from the crooked chimney. In many ways it looked like Number Four, Wigless Square. The sagging walls and lopsided, thatched roof were the same. There were, however, small differences. Number Four, Wigless Square, did not—as far as Alfie could remember—have a dead crow hanging over the front door by one foot. The roof hadn't actually caved in in places. Neither did Alfie remember a body crashing through the window of Number Four, Wigless Square, and sprawling unconscious in the road. 'Or—y'know— grubs and roots would be fine,' he added.

CHAPTER NINE

A NIGHT AT THE DEAD CROW

Another unconscious man lay spreadeagled on the floor inside the inn. The other customers were using him as a footrest. There were four of them, each with a collection of scars that made them look like they'd been patched together from whatever had been on special offer in the meat aisle at the supermarket. Leather, leering grins, and wicked-looking weaponry were very much in fashion. Teeth were not. None of the customers looked as menacing as the man behind the bar though. The innkeeper wore a torn leather waistcoat and a stained leather apron. A few sprigs of frightened-looking hair clung to the parts of his head that weren't covered in scars. One eye was covered by a patch. What really caught Alfie's attention though was the fact that one of his ears was on backwards. It was a different size to his other ear, too, and a mouldy colour, leading Alfie to think that the barman had lost his own ear in a fight and simply found someone else's before sewing it on without bothering to use a mirror. This was, in fact, exactly what had happened.

With a gulp, Alfie did his best not to stare. The barman didn't look like the type who would enjoy people staring at him. Keeping his gaze well away from the side of the man's head, Alfie sat on the stool closest to the miserable fire. He glanced at the Professor, and was horrified to see the old man *was* staring at the innkeeper's ear. His stomach sank. Any moment the Professor was going to say something that would get them both thrown out the window.

'Barf tolet cur-huggh neep blurt chutney,' the barman said.

The Professor spun the handle on the tiny

gramophone around his neck.

'Gurrgh. . . lcome to The Dead Crow, gentlemen,' the innkeeper continued in a voice that still sounded like a cement mixer full of bricks. 'What valuables might we tear from your bleeding bodies? Har har, I mean, what can I get for you?'

Alfie held his breath as the Professor began to speak.

'A beer for me, please. My young friend will have a lemonade,' said the Professor, taking a seat on a wobbling stool. He shot a look at Alfie. 'Packet of nuts while we look at the menu?'

Alfie nodded, letting his breath out. Even the Professor wasn't idiotic enough to mention the barman's weird ear.

'And a packet of nuts,' the Professor said to the barman. 'Oh, and the menu if you'd be so kind.' There was a pause, then he added, happily, 'I see you have a woman's ear badly sewn to the side of your head.'

The silence that fell was broken only by Alfie's petrified squeak.

'You can tell it's a *woman's* ear because it's

slightly smaller than a man's ear,' continued the Professor, who hadn't noticed the deadly quiet. 'Some sort of local tradition, is it? Exchanging ears as a love token I expect. These simple folk traditions are so interesting . . .'

'Are you trying to be *funny*?' interrupted the innkeeper, cracking his knuckles. 'Only, last week someone else tried being funny and I had to pull. His. Head. Off. We don't *like* people being funny, do we lads?'

The Dead Crow's other customers growled in agreement.

'Have I said something wrong?' the Professor asked, looking around.

'Please,' Alfie cut in, winding the handle on his own translator. 'We don't want any trouble. My friend is just a bit . . . um . . . *odd*. Don't take any notice of anything he says. Just the ear . . . I mean *beer* . . . and lemonade and nuts . . . *please*.'

'Ain't got no lemonade, ain't got no lar-di-dar nuts. Got beer and stew.'

'Then one beer, one glass of water, and two stews . . . thank you very much,' said Alfie.

'And you'll be wanting to buy a round of beers for everyone else, too, I reckon,' growled the innkeeper, leaning over him.

'Yes, drinks all round,' said Alfie, nervously.

'That's more like it,' said the innkeeper, busying himself behind the counter. 'Here we are then. One water, one pint of my *finest* beer. Plus what everyone else is drinking. That'll be *fifty* gold shillings.' He slammed two filthy tankards in front of Alfie, winking at the group of cut-throats at the table behind.

Alfie peered into the tankards. The contents of both were the same brown, muddy colour. Both smelt like cat pee.

'That's *very* expensive,' spluttered the Professor. From the breast pocket of his jacket he pulled an embroidered purse and emptied it on to the counter. Alfie counted seven pounds and twenty-eight pence in loose change, two sequins, what looked like a dried sprout, and some fluff.

'We also accept payment in all major blood types,' growled the innkeeper.

Alfie squeezed his eyes closed and sighed. The

innkeeper was trying to rip them off. Alfie didn't know what fifty gold coins were worth in pounds and pence but it was certainly more than the price of six pints of cat pee. For the second time that day he was in life-threatening danger. He was getting really, *really* fed up with his adventure and starting to think that all the books he had read had been lying to him. According to them, an inn like this should have been full of apple-cheeked locals singing and dancing on the tables, whole boars roasting over roaring fires, and maybe a hooded stranger sitting alone in the corner. He'd had enough. Opening his eyes, he put his hand over the Professor's pile of coins and said, quietly, 'Actually, we won't be paying, Mr . . . aah?'

'My name ain't Mr Aah,' grunted the innkeeper. 'It's Gerald. Gerald Teethcrusher.'

'Then we won't be paying, Mr *Teethcrusher*,' Alfie said.

'Oh dear, oh dear, oh *dear*,' grinned Gerald Teethcrusher. 'What a shame. Only you've looked at your drinks now, ain't you? Can't serve 'em to anyone else. Blood it is then.'

Alfie heard stools scrape as The Dead Crow's other customers got to their feet behind him— except the man on the floor, who just twitched. Metal sighed against leather as weapons were drawn. From beneath his counter, Gerald Teethcrusher pulled a length of wood sprouting nails. 'Now look ear . . .' the Professor began.

Alfie silenced him with a nudge, and pulled the notebook from his pocket. 'Tell me, Mr Teethcrusher,' he said, quietly. 'Have you ever heard the words "restaurant review"?'

'No, but I heard the words "woman's ear", and I ain't having that,' replied Teethcrusher, giving his length of wood a test swing. It whipped past Alfie's nose with a horrible, rusty, swishing sound.

'I ripped this ear fresh off Wilfred the Berserk, I did. It's just shrunk a bit is all.'

'Let me explain,' said Alfie.

'So, have I got this right?' Teethcrusher said, ten minutes later. 'I give you free food and drink and a bed for the night and you'll put a whatjamacallit . . .'

'Review,' said Alfie, helpfully.

'A *reee-vew*,' the barman continued, testing the word. 'You'll put a reee-vew in this book what you're doin'.'

'*The Cosmic Atlas*,' Alfie nodded, tapping the leather-bound book with his pencil. 'Everyone who reads it will know they'll find a great Outlandish welcome at Gerald Teethcrusher's Dead Crow, with a friendly atmosphere and a tasty bowl of stew at a price to suit any pocket.'

'And if I break your legs and throw you out the window?'

'Then I'll be forced to write that The Dead Crow is an expensive, filthy, stinking, rathole packed with villainous scum.'

'I ain't villainous scum most of the time. I'm a hairdresser,' said one of the customers behind Alfie. 'I'm only villainous scum in the evenings.'

'Shut your face, Manly Todd,' Teethcrusher snapped. Alfie could almost see the innkeeper's mind whirring. 'So, if you wrote *nice* things, people'll read it and say to themselves, "hullo, that place looks smashin', I'll go spend me money there"?'

Alfie nodded. 'Maybe you could do the place up a bit. Call it "Thank Goodness it's Teethcrusher's". Serve stew made to your own secret recipe.'

'I could have a dining area with me souvenirs up on the wall,' said Teethcrusher. 'Me collection of blunt objects and teeth.'

'That would look . . . err . . . great,' said Alfie. 'Really great. You'd probably make enough to open another inn in no time, then another and another. You'd have more gold than you could spend.'

'Ooh, I could get the leather shorts I've been

wanting. With the studs. Well . . . maybe I was a little bit hasty with you gentlemen,' Teethcrusher replied. He pushed the two tankards closer. 'I'll just go and make your beds up and see about that stew then. Funny you should say, but it *is* my very own secret recipe.'

'Really?' said Alfie.

'Yeah, I bit off one of Manly Todd's fingers last week and spat it in. Din't I do that, Manly?'

'You did that, Gerald Teethcrusher,' answered Manly Todd. 'That were my curling tong finger, too.'

As Gerald Teethcrusher stomped away, the Professor turned to Alfie. 'Rupert, my boy,' he whispered. 'I . . . ah . . . I admire your . . . um . . . quick thinking. Of course I do. But I did tell you that I'm only having *one* copy of *The Cosmic Atlas* printed, didn't I?'

'You did,' said Alfie, 'And I didn't tell Mr Teethcrusher any different.'

'Even so, the Unusual Cartography Club is a serious research institute. We . . . ah . . . we don't put *reviews* in our books. That's not the way we do things. Might as well make the *Atlas* some kind of gaudy travel guide. Or start taking money to put in advertisements. And then where would we be?'

Alfie thought about it. 'A lot richer?' he said. 'Not being thrown out of your headquarters?' Shrugging, he took a swig from his tankard, then spat the contents of his mouth on the floor. Picking up his pencil, he started to write . . .

MIDELYSIA: WHERE TO STAY

The Dead Crow *****

No visit to Outlandish's Midelysian region
would be complete without a visit to
Gerald Teethcrusher's famous inn, The
Dead Crow. Oozing rustic, olde worlde,
pull-your-head-off charm, you'll find
whatever you're looking for here, so
long as you're looking for a fight and/
or explosive diarrhoea. With a menu that
will suit the food-lover with a taste for
danger, The Dead Crow is bound to leave
you with treasured memories, stomach
parasites, and—very likely—serious head
wounds.

CHAPTER TEN
A WEIRDO CALLS AT MIDNIGHT

Both Alfie and the Professor took one sniff of the stew and stuck to stale bread and mouldy cheese. By the time the embers in the fire grate had gone out they were both yawning. Wishing Manly Todd and his villainous friends good night, the two of them followed Gerald Teethcrusher up a creaky flight of stairs to the guest room. 'Where's the bathroom?' asked Alfie, peering around at blood-stained walls and the straw-stuffed sacks. The sacks were slowly moving across the floor but Alfie decided they must be beds because the room contained nothing else that looked like it might be a bed. In fact, it contained nothing else at all, apart from a horrible smell.

Teethcrusher stopped to beat the sacks with a broom, and stood back, satisfied, when they stopped moving. 'Fleas,' he explained. 'At no extra cost. You might want to put that in yer ree-vew.' Pointing to the tiny window, he added 'Toilet. We ask our customers not to use it when someone is walking by underneath, but it's a laugh if you do.'

It was a dump but Alfie was too tired to care. As soon as Teethcrusher slammed the door he fell onto a sack, pulled another sack up to his nose, and quickly fell asleep while the Professor grumbled about putting a review in *The Cosmic Atlas*. Soon, even his muttering trailed off and the room was silent except for the gentle rustle of stunned fleas.

An hour or two later the window creaked open.

Alfie awoke to a pricking beneath his chin. Thinking it was a flea, he tried to brush it way and found he couldn't move. His arms were pinned to the floor. A weight on his chest stopped him moving. 'Baa botham t'ch Skingrath. Gusset maasdam banana,' a voice hissed, though Alfie could hardly hear it above the Professor's honking snores.

Reluctantly, he opened one eye. In a shaft of moonlight coming in through the window, he saw a dark figure sitting on his chest. The point of a dagger pressed against his throat. The figure was dressed in stinking animal skins. It was probably a girl, he decided, because she had long hair, though she could have done with a visit to Manly Todd. It was matted into dreadlocks, while her face was covered in mud and old paint. Groaning, 'Gerroff,' Alfie shut his eye again and tried to roll over.

The pricking became more painful. 'Baa botham t'ch Skingrath. Gusset maasdam *banana*,' the girl repeated.

Somewhere in Alfie's sleepy brain a voice explained to him that one of the Children of Skingrath had him pinned to the bed and was holding a knife to his throat. Even though he was getting thoroughly bored of people threatening to kill him, the voice told him, it was still the sort of thing to which he should give his full attention.

Both Alfie's eyes snapped open. 'Eh . . . eh . . . wh-what's going on?' he gurgled. 'Who are *you*?'

'*Baa botham t'ch Skingrath. Gusset maasdam*

banana,' hissed the girl for the third time, sounding angrier this time.

'Oh right, I'm going to need the translator,' he croaked. He tried nodding towards the gramophone that he'd put on the floor beside his bed but stopped when the point of the girl's knife pressed harder against his skin. 'No understando,' he said slowly, rolling his eyes towards the translator. 'Need magic boxo.'

Warily, the girl shifted her weight, allowing Alfie to reach for the box while keeping her knife point pressed to his skin. He turned the handle, winding up the mechanism inside. 'Now,' he said, nervously, 'is there something I can help you with?'

'You and the false Skingrath deceived us. You shall both die,' the girl hissed.

'Well, sorry but we didn't have much choice. You *were* going to sacrifice us and . . . wait . . . "banana" means "die" in Outlandish?'

'Yes.'

'Funny old universe,' Alfie murmured to himself. The girl lifted her knife to strike.

'Hey! Stop that!' Alfie croaked. 'Let me explain!'

'You deceived my people, false Rupert. What is there to explain?'

'For a start, my name's , not Rupert, it's Alfie.'

'See? Even your name is a lie.' The girl held the knife higher.

'This is all a misunderstanding,' Alfie babbled. 'There *is* no Skingrath. Well there might be, but if *he's* a god so is the old man over there. He's worshipped on fourteen worlds. There's a statue of him. Seventy metres high.'

The girl paused. 'You tell me that the old fool whose face is like that of the Pathetic Wanja Bird really *is* a god?' she whispered. 'I do not believe you.'

'No,' Alfie said, quickly. 'I'm saying the circle of stones wasn't a shrine, it was a gateway to other worlds. Maybe some weirdo thingy with three heads, tusks, and fiery hair might have come through it by accident and *told* your ancestors it was a god, but the Wanja-faced old man isn't a god and neither was Skingrath.' After a second, he added, 'Probably.' After all, he hadn't met Skingrath personally and he was learning that the universe was full of surprises. For all he knew, Skingrath might be the Easter Bunny.

Bathed in moonlight, the Child of Skingrath held

still, breathing heavily. 'More lies,' she hissed after a while. 'Skingrath is a real god. He watches over us.'

'Oh really?' said Alfie. 'Drops by all the time, does he?'

'I will beat you to death with your own lungs.' The girl glared down. The point of the knife twitched, dangerously.

At this point the Professor turned over, mumbling in his sleep, 'Why thank you, Aunt Lucy, but I'll sleep in the garden. My knees smell of peanuts, you see.' This didn't really help Alfie with the difficult situation he found himself in and is only mentioned here to keep the story accurate.

'I'm telling the truth,' Alfie went on, urgently. 'If the circle wasn't a gateway how do you think *we* arrived?'

Again, the girl hesitated. 'No,' she said. 'The old man is Jael the Deceiver and you are a demon. Jealous of Skingrath, the two of you destroyed His holy place.'

'Actually I sort of pushed it over by accident,' Alfie told her. 'Bit of a disaster, really. We have to find another circle so we can get home.'

'Another?' The girl lowered her knife a centimetre. 'You seek another shrine?'

'Yes,' said Alfie, nodding, 'Hey, why don't you come with us? You can see for yourself. You might even get to meet Skingrath.'

As soon as the words left his mouth he knew they'd been a mistake. He'd only meant to lighten the mood, which was—in his opinion—far too stabby. Instead, the girl said, 'You know of a way to use Skingrath's shrine to travel to His realm? You will show me the path?'

'Um . . . yeah . . . well . . . the path, maybe. Not actually, like, going with you or anything,' Alfie stammered.

Ignoring him, the Skingrathian girl blinked, then she nodded sternly, and said, 'Then I *shall* join your quest. Lead me to this shrine. If what you say is true I will . . . I will . . . seek out Skingrath and bring word of him to my people. You will be rewarded with your lives. If your words are false then I shall cut out your stomach and wear it as a hat during the rainy season.'

'Oh . . . er . . . right,' said Alfie. 'Welcome to

team Unusual Cartography Club, I suppose. Sorry, I didn't catch your name . . .'

'My name is Hunter-Of-The-Vicious-Spiny-Dereko-Beast,' said the girl.

'Pleased to meet you, Hunter-Of . . .'

'You may call me Derek.'

'Sorry Aunt Lucy, I can't talk now. I'm inside a tomato,' the Professor mumbled. 'I . . . oh . . . er . . . who's this? Aren't you going to introduce me, Rupert?'

Alfie and Derek turned their heads to find the Professor had awoken. Sitting up on his pile of sacks, he rubbed his eyes and peered through the gloom.

'This is . . . um . . . Derek,' said Alfie.

'You've made a friend, eh?' the Professor said, beaming. 'And now you're having a midnight wrestle, I see. Takes me back to the old days at the UCC when me and the lads shared a room. One night, Jimmy Whuppley . . .'

'Derek's coming with us,' Alfie interrupted.

'Is he? Is he *really*?' The Professor looked bewildered. 'Ah, why would he do that exactly?'

'I seek Skingrath,' Derek growled. 'And if you should attempt to stop me or destroy another of His shrines then I shall put you on a spike and leave you for the Hunger Ants.'

CHAPTER ELEVEN

THE ROAD TO VERMINIUM

The Professor scratched his chin while Alfie refilled Betsy's petrol tank. The moped was almost hidden beneath the pile of baggage. 'She's a bit overloaded already, Rupert,' he said. 'Not sure where your new pal is going to sit.'

Holding her chin up proudly, Derek said, 'Of all the Children of Skingrath, I am the best hunter and runner in the under-sixteens category. I have no need to ride your foolish metal horse, pitiful false god.'

'Oh, right,' said the Professor, out loud. From the corner of his mouth he whispered to Alfie, 'Not very friendly, is he? Are you *sure* you want to bring him along?'

Alfie shrugged. 'She said she'd sew our eyelids to our bottoms if we refused,' he whispered back.

'I see,' huffed the Professor. 'Well, I suppose that settles it. All aboard then. Verminium here we come.'

After tying the can of petrol onto the luggage, Alfie climbed into Betsy's saddle quickly, eager to be on the road and on his way home before his mum got home from work. Strapping on his helmet, he gave Gerald Teethcrusher a farewell wave. Hoping for a flood of new customers once Alfie's review was published, Teethcrusher was making changes to The Dead Crow. The worst of the dried sick had been chipped off the floor and he'd made a sign advertising 'Romantik Brakes at The *Faymus* Ded Crowe'. The innkeeper was now building a kiddies' play area, which—as far as Alfie could see—meant digging a hole in the ground and filling it with rusty bear traps.

Betsy chugged off towards the rising sun. Glancing back around the mound of baggage,

Alfie watched Derek break into a run. She soon caught up with the moped, loping alongside Alfie and the Professor with bow and arrow bouncing on her shoulder, dreadlocks flowing in the breeze, and a look of fierce determination on her painted face. Deciding he should try to make friends with their new companion, Alfie spun the handle on his translator and shouted, 'So . . . um . . . Derek . . . won't your mum and dad miss you?'

Derek glared at him for a moment, then looked away. 'The woman who gave birth to me left me in the mountains when I was six winters old,' she replied, sounding distant. 'I was not allowed to return to my people until I had survived a full three winters fighting off wild beasts in the dreary wilderness, armed with only a stick. By the time I returned . . .'

'I had a similar experience,' the Professor interrupted. 'Got lost, funnily enough on the Lost World of Lost. Four *years* I wandered about. I didn't have a stick, of course. Had to eat moss. Plus, the local people bundled me into in a sack and threw me in a pond every week. Never did find out why.'

Feeling a little left out, Alfie said, 'Me and my mum are so poor we only ever eat fish-head soup.'

Derek grunted. 'I once ate my own toenails.'

'Delicious,' said the Professor. 'I had to eat my own dandruff once. It's not as bad as you might think.'

'Well, it's not really *soup*,' Alfie chipped in. 'More like brown water with fish heads floating about. The neighbours are always complaining about the smell.'

'Would you like to try some dandruff?' the Professor asked him. 'It's quite fresh.'

'Maybe later,' Alfie replied. 'How about you, Derek? Some dandruff for breakfast?'

'Enough talk,' Derek spat. 'This mindless gossip angers me.'

'So, they won't miss you then, your mum and dad?' Alfie asked, after a few more minutes of bouncing along the muddy track.

'Do not speak to me. You are weak and strange. I do not like you.' Derek glared at him again, and increased her pace until she was beyond hearing distance.

With a shrug, Alfie pulled his notebook from the saddlebag and began to make notes as well as he could while Betsy bounced along the Great Verminium Road towards Outlandish's greatest city. Along the way they made a few stops to update *The Cosmic Atlas*. Alfie also jotted down some information about the places they visited . . .

DISCOVERING . . . THE GREAT VERMINIUM ROAD

Winding through the foothills of the Hambanjo Mountains, the Great Verminium Road is one of Outlandish's most scenic and difficult roads. Be warned, there are some accident black spots where you might be delayed by a pile-up of goats. The splendid mountain views make the trip worthwhile though, and there are many interesting places to visit along the way, including . . .

THE SHRINE OF HERSOOT THE HAIRY

Visitors to the shrine are said to receive Hersoot's blessing of a thick and impressive beard. Unfortunately, it is only open to women. The site also has a small museum, which—for some reason—is devoted to the history of gum disease.

BLADDER CASTLE

Built by King Uryan the Damp, one of Outlandish's least popular kings, the ruined Bladder Castle has one bedroom but three-hundred-and-twenty-seven toilets. It is said that King Uryan never made it to any of them.

POTATO FIELD

What looks like a field of potatoes is actually the site of a famous battle. Here, Verminium's greatest soldier, General Mayhem, and his army did battle with an evil sorcerer who turned them all into potatoes. A roadside shack now offers hungry travellers baked potatoes.

THE ANNOYING CHICKEN OF KENTARN

This amazing sculpture of a giant chicken was built by a forgotten tribe of ancient folk. When the wind is in the right direction the chicken actually sings. Sadly, the ancient folk had no taste in music and the local people are now often kept awake by the statue droning *Balzug's Pig Is An Ugly Pig*, except when the wind is from the south-west when it just makes loud farting noises.

As the day wore on, the landscape changed again. Woods and hills gave way to fields filled with green stuff. As a city boy, Alfie had never seen anything like it but decided these might be farms and jotted that down. As morning passed into afternoon single farmhouses became small villages. The sight of people became more common and a question began to form in Alfie's mind. The people were—without a doubt—people. He glanced ahead to where Derek was running. She, too, had two arms, two legs, one head, and—Alfie assumed —all the usual attachments and thingummybobs: armpits, a bellybutton, toenails, and so on. It was puzzling. Leaning forwards, he pointed with his pencil and shouted at the Professor's crash-helmet, 'Those are people. Plus, that's a cow, isn't it?' He'd seen pictures of cows in books and felt on fairly safe ground.

'Well spotted,' said the Professor. 'That is indeed a cow. The people are, in fact, people. Top marks for observation.'

'Yes, but *why*?' said Alfie. 'Why aren't they weird aliens with pointy heads, or little green cows? Why do people and cows look the same as they do on Earth?'

'Oh, people have been hopping about the universe for a long time,' said the Professor with a wave of his hand that made Betsy wobble dangerously. Gripping the handlebars again, he continued. 'The legends say a man called Partley Mildew invented the first stone circle about a million years ago on a planet called Wip-Bop-a-Looma, starting a craze for intergalactic travel. Humans slowly spread out across the universe, building more and more circles and jumping from one world to another in search of a relaxing break in the sunshine. In fact, most of the human worlds started out as a holiday destinations.'

To take another short break from the story it's worth mentioning that the Professor was absolutely right: stone circles are the reason there are so many humans around the universe. After they were invented by Partley Mildew, humans used them to discover thousands of new worlds, building more circles wherever they went. This was known as the Great Exploration Period, during which many clubs and cartography societies sprung up around the universe. After a while though, humans became bored with stone circles. It was widely agreed that once you've seen a few thousand worlds you've seen pretty much everything there is to see. So people settled down on the worlds they liked best and—after a while—forgot about the stone circles. This is why there are so many humans across the universe but only a few planets are inhabited by, say, the Ghastly Snailprod beings of the Andromeda Galaxy. Most alien species have not discovered circles and are forced to use spaceships. Spaceships are, of course, a very slow and dull way to get around.

'Did you say, *holiday* destinations?' Alfie asked.

'Oh yes. There was a big surge in tourism that lasted thousands and thousands of years. The UCC's books say that's how human life on Earth began. Very popular in its day, the Earth.'

'So, we're all descended from alien tourists?' Alfie babbled, feeling like everything he'd learned was wrong. He'd spent an entire term at school studying evolution, and that was eight weeks

wasted. 'How could we not *know* something like
that?'

'Oh, you'd be amazed what people forget,' the
Professor said with a shrug. 'Just look at pyramids.'

'What *about* pyramids?' Alfie asked.

Sadly, this question must go unanswered. At
that moment Derek stopped at the top of a hill.
With a squeal of brakes, the Professor pulled Betsy
up beside her.

Alfie gaped.

Spread out across a valley below them, was
a city. A ribbon of grey river wound through the
centre. A palace squatted like a toad on its bank.
Spires and towers rose from the huddled rooftops.
Flags and pennants snapped from battlements.
Screams wafted up on the smoke from burning
buildings.

All this was just background though. The
city could have been made of hair and Alfie still
wouldn't have spared it a glance. He was far too
busy gawping at the dragon that soared above
it. Glimmering crimson, its scales sparkled in the
sunlight as it rolled and twisted through the air,

wings beating with great thumps. Now and again it roared a torrent of flame and another building would disappear in a fiery blast while the screams grew louder.

Speechless, Alfie gazed at the creature. It was a dream and a nightmare. Something from one of his books made heart-stoppingly real. He tried to speak, his jaw working up and down, but only a choked gurgle came out. All the while, the dragon sprayed fire on the city below.

And then it was over. The dragon circled the city, catching the heat from the fires it had caused beneath its wings. With one, lazy, flip, it turned and glided away towards the horizon, leaving behind the fires of dragon breath.

'Ah,' said the Professor. 'This will be Verminium, I expect.'

CHAPTER TWELVE
DIRTY OLD TOWN

Verminium was cloaked in dingy shadow. Its streets were narrow, filthy, and filled with smoke. Tall, thatched houses blotted out the rest of the sunshine. Betsy puttered through crowds of people putting out fires. To Alfie's amazement there were also plenty of shoppers and street traders going about their business as if the city hadn't just been attacked by a giant, fire-breathing lizard. Clearly, the city was used to the dragon's visits.

No one spared the three travellers a glance. Anyone who wasn't fighting fires was busy with everyday city life. Shady characters lurked in side alleys, fingering daggers hidden beneath their cloaks. Young men threw up outside inns. People emptied rubbish and buckets out of windows. Scribbling furiously in his notebook, when he wasn't spinning the handle of his translator, Alfie passed a plump fortune-teller peering at a customer's hand. He caught the words, '. . . a dark, handsome stranger will rub your legs with cheese, Mrs Ointment . . .' Outside a shop filled with coffins, a man bellowed, 'Come to Dead Cosy. Coffins for all occasions, especially funerals.' Elsewhere, he heard anvils ringing against a background of wood being sawed, squealed swear-words, the squeak of leather, the screams of mugging victims, and the endless rise and fall of city babble.

To his own surprise, Alfie felt almost at home in the alien city. 'It's very different from the city back home, but oddly similar,' he said. 'Sort of like our city but a long time ago.'

'Well, yes,' nodded the Professor. 'People coming and going through the circles meant all sorts of ideas spread around the universe: building styles, clothes, sausages, and whatnot. Stories, too. That's why everyone knows about dragons even though there have never been any on Earth.'

DISCOVERING . . . VERMINIUM

They say that if you're tired of Verminium you're tired of being robbed. The city certainly has its fair share of muggers, con-artists, pickpockets, bag-snatchers, cheats, burglars, and general thieves. It's best to keep your valuables hidden at all times, preferably in a completely different city. But Verminium has a lot more than crime to offer, especially if you're a fan of open sewers.

It's worth interrupting again to point out that the Professor was only *mostly* right here. When humans spread out across the universe during the Great Exploration Period they did indeed carry with them stories and ideas. So on many human worlds there are castles, houses, and similar stories, as well the same designs for comfortable underwear. *Some* human worlds have, however, gone their own way since people stopped using circles. On the planet of Mumsy for instance, people live in the glurpal pouches of mountain-sized, twelve-legged Twang Bears and wear underwear made of concrete. Right, back to the story . . .

Two donkeys collided in the street ahead, stopping traffic. While their owners punched each other a familiar smell made Alfie's nose twitch. Turning, he saw a woman about his mum's age selling fish-head soup from a bubbling cauldron. Feeling suddenly more homesick than ever, he tore his gaze away and shouted 'Where next?' at the back of the Professor's helmet.

'Ah, I suppose we should ask around,' replied the Professor, staring around at the seething streets. 'I . . . er . . . There could be a library, I suppose, but I'm afraid I don't know where.'

'If only *The Cosmic Atlas* was some sort of gaudy travel guide,' Alfie sighed.

The Professor raised his voice, yelling at a man walking by, 'Er . . . hello . . . *hello* . . . yes, *you* sir with the dangly warts. Could you direct us to a library or a map-maker?'

'I'll direct you to my fist in a second.' Shaking his

warts, the man stalked off.

The Professor tried again. 'I say madam, I'm trying to find . . .'

'I know what you're trying to find,' the brightly dressed woman said, pulling the Professor's face to hers by the moustache. 'It's a kiss, isn't it? You're so handsome though. How could I resist?'

'Um . . . no actually. Er . . . would you mind taking your hand out of my pocket? Madam, *madam*! Stop that!'

'Ha,' chuckled the woman as she flounced off, tucking the Professor's purse into her blouse.

Derek drew her knife. 'My turn,' she said. 'I will torture one of these unbelievers until they give us the knowledge we seek.' Before Alfie could stop her, she had the front of a man's shirt in her hand and her knife to his throat. 'The path to the Shrine of Skingrath,' she hissed. 'Tell us how to find it.'

The man coughed. 'Ugh,' he said. 'You smell *awful*.'

'The *shrine*,' Derek repeated.

'Look, stinky, I've been robbed three times already this morning. I am *not* in the mood.'

'Where is the . . .' Derek started, her voice dripping with menace.

'That's enough, Derek,' Alfie interrupted. 'Let me try.'

Derek released the man. '*You?*' she sneered at Alfie. 'What can *you* do?'

'Watch and learn,' Alfie told her. Reaching out, he tugged at the skirt of the fish-head soup woman. 'Nice fish heads,' he said.

The woman shot him a smile. 'Want a bowl? It's cheap.'

'Er, no thanks,' said Alfie.

'Disgusting, ain't it?' the woman sighed. 'It's the eyes. They stare at you like it's all your fault. No one ever wants any.'

'Why don't you try selling something else?' Alfie asked.

'Like what?' the woman said, sounding gloomy. 'The dragon flies in every fortnight and threatens to burn the whole place down unless we send it gold. No one's got any money for decent food. Katy's Fried Moths already does moths, and old Dirtfinger over there—he's the one scratching his backside—

he does boiled trotters and snouts. The Cabbage King does cabbage, and that's all anyone can afford.'

Alfie thought about it for a moment, then spun the handle of his translator furiously. 'Can you get your hands on some flour?' he asked, 'and a few tomatoes and a little bit of cheese?'

The woman nodded.

'OK then,' he said. 'Roll some dough into a thin circle. Spread a little bit of tomato sauce on it. Add some grated cheese and then bake it in the oven for a few minutes. It's cheap to make and I promise people will buy it.'

The woman stared at him. 'I might just try that,' she said. 'I'll call it a bread-circle-with-tomato-sauce-and-cheese.'

'Or pizza,' said Alfie.

'Pizza.' the woman repeated. 'Yes, I like that.'

'*Everyone* likes pizza,' Alfie told her. 'And you can put extra toppings on, if you like.'

'I suppose I could talk to Katy,' said the woman. 'Pizza topped with moths might be tasty. Thanks son. Sure you don't want some soup? It's horrible.'

'No, really,' said Alfie. 'I'd rather eat dandruff.

But while we're chatting, we're looking for a stone circle. Could you possibly tell us where we might find some maps of Outlandish? Or a stone circle information centre or something?'

The fish woman tilted her head, thinking. 'You could ask at Sir Brenda's Valiant Quests. Dunno if they've got any maps but Sir Brenda's been everywhere, they say. It's on the bridge. Look for the suit of armour in the shop window.'

'Thanks, and the bridge is where?'

'Keep going down this street, you'll come to it.' As the moped puttered away, she called out, 'And if you come this way again come and get a pizza. Just ask for Domino. Domino Hutt.'

Alfie turned back to see Derek staring. 'It's called being polite,' he said. 'Which involves showing people what is known as "respect". Using this simple technique you will find people might "like" you and tell you what you want to know.'

With a grunt, Derek turned her head away.

'Well done, Rupert,' shouted the Professor. 'I see I shall have to give you a raise in pay!'

Betsy trundled on. The Professor steered

carefully through a group of ragged children, who immediately tried to make off with the baggage. Still sulking, Derek chased them off.

After a little while the old man cleared his throat. 'Ah, Rupert,' he said.

'Alfie,' said Alfie, although he had given up any real hope of the Professor remembering his name.

'You do understand that when I said I would raise your pay that was just a way of saying that you had done well, don't you? I mean I would if I could but you know I'm not *actually* giving you a pay rise?'

Alfie patted his shoulder. 'It's all right Professor, I know. Look, there's the bridge.'

DISCOVERING . . . THE OLD VERMINIUM BRIDGE

No visit to Verminium would be complete without taking in the sights at the Old Verminium Bridge. Built during the reign of Grand King Larceny VIII it was considered the greatest feat of engineering in Outlandish history until the gate tower collapsed on the king during the opening ceremony. It remains one of the city's most dangerous tourist attractions. Along its span, houses and shops tilt out over the river below at terrifying angles. Occasionally, blocks of stone drop off, sinking boats beneath.

Sir Blenda's Valiant Quests

CHAPTER THIRTEEN

SIR BRENDA'S VALIANT QUESTS

'Ah-ha, this must be the place,' said the Professor, coming to a stop outside a shop front. The sign over the door was faded and cracked and Alfie couldn't read it anyway, but a rusty suit of armour stood in the window. A tattered poster was pinned to the wall. It showed a woman in armour holding a glowing blue sword. In the background was a dark, goblin-infested fortress.

A bell tinkled when Alfie pushed the door open, then came loose and fell on his head. Alfie put it on a nearby shelf while Derek squeezed through the door with the Professor close behind. Behind a counter stood a handsome man with blond hair and a wailing baby on his hip. Glancing over, he said, 'Be with you in a moment, I'm just dealing with this gentleman.'

The little shop already had a customer: a red-faced man wearing a dented breastplate and a helmet with a spike on top. 'Eeeeeyes *front*,' he bellowed, stamping his feet and saluting. 'Forsooth and verily, and all that sort of thing, let it be known that Lord Spittelgrad, our most glorious Oppressor, does seek an adventurer to undertake a daring quest on behalf of this fair city. Said adventurer will be richly rewarded.'

'You can lower your voice, Sergeant Pillage,' said the man behind the counter. 'I'm not deaf.'

'It's all part of being a sergeant is shouting, Mister Herkleton,' the sergeant said, in a voice still loud enough to make the windows rattle.

'*Prince* Herkleton,' the man corrected.

'Sorry, your prince-i-ness.'

'I wonder what this is all about,' Alfie whispered.

'Is this about that dragon again, Pillage?' said Prince Herkleton while jiggling the baby up and down. 'I've told you a hundred times my wife's away on a quest so she can't help.'

'Er . . . that's . . . um . . . well, it *might* be about the dragon,' Pillage bawled. 'But Sir Brenda's been away on a quest for the last three *years*. When's she coming back?'

'Oh, you know what quests are like,' said the prince. 'She's probably battling some goblin horde. Could take a while.'

'You'll be sure to tell her about the rich rewards when she gets back though?'

'And what are they this time? Please do tell.'

'Our beloved Oppressor, Lord Spittelgrad, offers the hand of his daughter, the almost lovely Daphne, in marriage.'

'Does he? Does he *really*?' said Prince. 'I wonder what Daphne thinks of that. Only she's seventy-six now. There's also the small fact that Sir Brenda is already married. To me.'

'There's a mountain of gold up for grabs, too,' added the sergeant.

'Sergeant Pillage, Lord Spittelgrad is a terrible old miser. It is well known that his mountain of gold is a tiny little model of a mountain. It's made of gold—yes—but it's no bigger than a mouse's nose.'

'It's a good model,' puffed the sergeant. 'Very skilled job getting all those crags right on a little model like that. Got to be worth a bit.'

'Is it worth my wife having her head burned off?' Prince Herkleton asked. 'Only that's what happened to the last twenty-six people what went off to fight the dragon.'

VERMINIUM'S PEOPLE . . .
LORD SPITTELGRAD: THE OPPRESSOR

Ruled by kings and queens for many centuries, Verminium's latest ruler is Lord Spittelgrad, known as the 'Oppressor.' Described as a 'nasty old git' by everyone who has ever met him, Lord Spittelgrad won the kingdom from the very stupid King Wibble in a card game called 'Twenty-One' where the players have to score as close to twenty-one without going over twenty-one. The king somehow managed to score 98,375.

'There's also the matter of civic pride,' Pillage argued. 'Someone could walk tall in this city after slaying the actual dragon.'

'Not without a head they couldn't.' The prince held up his free hand to stop the Sergeant's reply and continued. 'It doesn't matter anyway. As I said, she's not here, Pillage. Good day.'

'But . . . but . . .'

'I said, good *day*, sergeant,' the prince repeated. 'That means you go away now.'

Alfie watched with wide eyes as Sergeant Pillage barged past them and marched into the crowd. Venturing forth to slay dragons was *exactly* the sort of thing that happened in the books he loved. 'That sounds like a *great* quest,' he murmured to himself. 'I'd love to get a closer look at that dragon.'

Obviously, Alfie *was* destined to get a closer look at the dragon: a *much* closer look. That goes without saying. He just didn't know it yet. For the moment, the Professor nudged him and said, 'Sorry Rupert, but we already *have* a quest as you might remember. Returning you to your mum, eh? Best not to get sidetracked. I got sidetracked once, thinking it would be just a brief sidetrack. Then I got sidetracked from the sidetrack and before I knew it I was sidetracking here there and everywhere. Took me *ages* to get tracked again . . . What on Earth am I talking about?'

'We seek Skingrath, not dragons,' growled Derek.

'Do we?' asked the Professor, more confused than ever. 'I thought *I* was Skingrath.'

Alfie sighed. The Professor was right— about their quest at least—they couldn't go off adventuring after dragons when his mum might be worrying.

'Can I help you?' Prince Herkleton asked. 'Or did you just want to stand there chattering all day?'

'Good day to you,' said the Professor. 'I very much *hope* you can help us. We are here on a matter of bold adventure.'

'Well then, you're in the manky butter,' said the prince.

'Are we?' asked Alfie.

'Rats,' muttered the Professor, winding up the gramophone around his neck. 'Translator lost power. Would you mind repeating the last bit?'

'I said you're in the right place,' Prince Herkleton repeated. 'At Sir Brenda's Valiant Quests we pride ourselves on our bold adventures. Rescuing princes and princesses, beating back the forces of evil, finding treasure . . . *especially* finding treasure. What did you have in mind? There's a wicked overlord over Gibbett-Creaking way who needs vanquishing. It'd make a nice quest for beginners and my wife can show you the ropes: creeping into the dark fortress, escaping dungeons, locating and removing the treasure, and so on. Or there's a giant up near Demonhorn. Usually good for a bit of treasure, the giants . . .'

'But I thought Sir Brenda was already away on a quest,' said Alfie. 'Battling a goblin horde, you said.'

'Oh, *that*,' said the prince. 'That's just what I tell Sergeant Pillage. The Oppressor sends him down here every couple of months asking for my wife to go and fight the dragon. Have you ever *seen* a dragon?'

'Yes,' said Alfie, nodding. 'We saw it earlier. It was . . .'

'. . . an armour-plated, unkillable, fire-breathing, death machine,' the prince finished for him. 'And I will *not* allow my wife to go anywhere near it, especially not for a pinhead of gold and the hand of poor old Daphne in marriage.'

Feeling that the conversation was drifting off the point, Alfie said, 'We're looking for a circle of stones.'

Prince Herkleton raised an eyebrow as if to say, *call that a quest?* Out loud, he said. 'It's your adventure, I suppose. Our rates are fifty percent of any treasure found plus ten gold shillings per day, and expenses. My wife will expect dinner at six every night and a bed in a decent inn whenever possible. She gets cramp.'

'A sign of weakness,' sneered Derek.

Alfie elbowed her in the ribs, saying, 'We don't have any actual money. But I could put an advert for Sir Brenda's Valiant Quests in the book that . . .'

The rest of Alfie's sentence was drowned out by the Professor's outraged spluttering. '*Advertisements!*' he yelped.

'I see,' Prince Herkleton interrupted. 'No *actual* money. Any treasure at this stone circle?'

Alfie looked up at the Professor, who stopped spluttering long enough to shake his head. 'Probably not,' he admitted.

The prince rolled his eyes. 'Oh right,' he said. 'You're that type: all eager to be off on a quest and never mind that Sir Brenda's got six children to feed. Well, the door's behind you. I'd wish you luck with your quest but I don't really care. Good day.'

'But look here!' the Professor protested.

'That means go away,' the prince snapped. 'Why do I always have to explain that?'

Hearing Derek's knife slip from its sheath, Alfie elbowed her again. She muttered something about breaking his spine in three places. 'We were just hoping to have a few words with Sir Brenda,' he said, politely. 'Really, it will only take a few moments.'

'Get. Out.' The prince growled.

At that moment a voice from a back room roared, 'Herkleton! Herkleton, my own precious angel! What is it? Do we have a customer?'

'Oh rats,' yelped Sir Brenda's own precious angel.

SIR BRENDA'S VALIANT QUESTS

PROVIDING HAND–PICKED ADVENTURES
SINCE ABOUT TWENTY YEARS AGO.*

.... ▼ ....

Bored? Fed up with doing the same old job every day? Is there a daring adventurer inside you screaming to get out?

*At **Sir Brenda's Valiant Quests** we can help! Whether you dream of battling pirates on the high seas, slaughtering goblins in haunted mazes, or going one-on-one with a terrifying dreadlord, our experienced staff have the right quest for you. Choose from our fabulous range and receive a **FREE** enchanted sword with your first booking!**

ORDER YOUR CATALOGUE TODAY!

*Sword is for display purposes only and does not contain magic.

CHAPTER FOURTEEN

THE CIRCLE OF
THE CIRCLE

'*Customers*!' bawled Sir Brenda, slamming open the door from the back room and beaming around the room. 'Hurrah! Well met, fellows. When do we start our quest?'

'Sweetheart,' hissed her husband. '*I* deal with customers; *you* take care of the hero stuff. Aren't you supposed to be sharpening your sword.'

'My sword is already sharp, my one true love,' replied Sir Brenda, winking at her husband. 'All ready to stick into some skeleton ghoul or tentacle-headed monster from beyond our worst nightmares. So where are we off to? The blood-stained mines of Amun-Skrietch? The Black Gates of Howling

Oblivion? No, don't tell me yet. Come into the back and reveal your bold plan over ale and a pickled egg.'

Prince Herkleton groaned. '*Brenda*! We are *not* running a free restaurant!'

His wife held up a hand. 'Now, now, Herkleton, my sweet. This is quest business and there are *traditions*. Plotting in a smoky room over a mug of ale and a pickled egg is one of them.'

'You are *not* smoking that filthy pipe!' Herkleton snapped.

'Later, we shall lift our voices to sing sad songs,' Sir Brenda continued, 'before stealing off, cloaked and hooded, with our enemies hard on our heels. Now *that's* what I call questing.'

'We don't really have any enemies, I'm afraid,' the Professor chipped in.

'No enemies?' bellowed Sir Brenda. 'Then we shall *find* some, and they will regret the day they ever tangled with we four, who shall be known as the Fellowship of the . . . of the . . . what is it we're questing for?'

'We seek to return young Rupert here to his mum, Sir Brenda,' said the Professor.

'The Fellowship of Returning Young Rupert Here to his Mum,' said Sir Brenda, shaking her head. 'No, that doesn't work at all.'

'And Skingrath,' added Derek.

'The Fellowship of Skingrath?' said Sir Brenda. 'Hmmm. Better.'

'We're not too bothered about Skingrath, really,' said Alfie. 'Skingrath isn't at the top of our to-do list. But if you could possibly tell us where to find a ring of stones . . .'

'A ring of stones? A ring? Then we shall be the Fellowship of the *Ring*! Perfect.'

'Umm . . . I think that's already been done,' Alfie mumbled. He already liked Sir Brenda and didn't want to disappoint her. The knight filled the doorway with clanking armour, its rust matching her cloud of red hair. She grinned a lot, her light-reflecting teeth making the small shop noticeably brighter.

'Ah. How about the *Brothership of the Circle*? How does that sound?'

'Well, it's all right,' said Alfie, 'but you're female. So is Derek.'

'*Is* he?' said the Professor. 'Is he *really*?'

'Umm-hmm,' said Alfie.

'Takes all sorts, I suppose,' said the Professor. 'Never judge people, that's my motto. I mean, we all like slipping into a pair of tights now and then, don't we? And maybe a slinky off-the-shoulder dress. If you've got the figure for it, I always say . . .'

'*Professor*,' said Alfie, warningly.

'Ah yes,' said the Professor. 'Sidetracked. The quest, eh?'

Sir Brenda had been thinking hard. Lifting a finger in the air, she yelped, 'Got it! We'll be *The Circle of the Circle*! Hurrah! Now *that's* sorted we can have a sing and steal away into the night . . . I mean the late afternoon. Let me just fetch my hooded cloak.'

'Look, Sir Brenda, you don't need to come *with* us,' said Alfie.

'Oh.' Sir Brenda's grin vanished. 'That's a shame. We haven't had a customer in months.'

'You're sure you haven't got any money?' Prince Herkleton interrupted. 'I could let you have Sir Brenda for only five gold shillings a day.'

'And if you wanted a quest with a bit more zip I could do you a very exciting adventure seeking out the Enchanted Eyeball of Beelzebobby,' added Sir Brenda. 'It's got flesh-eating ghouls, gibbering hell-creatures, the lot.'

'Erm, no. Just the stone circle,' said the Professor.

'Or we could storm the Fortress of Endless Pain,' said Sir Brenda. 'Both *great* quests. I'll tell you what, special offer: buy one quest get the other free.'

'They sound great, but we're looking for a circle,' said Alfie.

Sir Brenda sighed. 'Oh, all right then. It sounds a bit dull though. What's so special about this circle?'

'It's just a stone circle,' said the Professor. 'Made of stones. Big ones.'

Sir Brenda frowned. 'I'd much rather battle mad gods.'

'Well if we do run into Skingrath, I understand he's always up for a fight,' said Alfie. 'We'd be happy to point him in your direction.'

'If we run into Skingrath he will destroy you all,' Derek grumped.

Everyone ignored her. No one needs that kind of

negativity.

'But really, we're just looking for a circle,' said Alfie. 'Only we're stuck in this world and it's my mum's birthday tomorrow, and . . . and . . .' Choking, he added, 'Please help us. If we can find a way to pay for your help, I promise we will.'

'No problem,' said Sir Brenda, waving a hand. 'There's a circle over that way. About two days' ride. Up in the mountains. Stoneygate, I think they call it.'

'Hm, yes,' said the Professor. 'That's where we came from. Bit of an accident I'm sorry to report. We sort of broke it. Do you know of any *other* stone circles?'

'No,' said Sir Brenda. 'I have quested everywhere in this land and I have never seen another stone circle.'

It was the last straw. Alfie felt tears welling in his eyes. His mum was lost forever.

'But that's *brilliant*,' continued Sir Brenda.

Alfie blinked. 'How *exactly* is it brilliant?' he asked.

Sir Brenda's eyes shone. 'It's brilliant,' she

roared, 'because now we have a proper *quest*! *The Circle of the Circle* shall seek out a circle. Wherever it lies and whatever horrors we must face, we *shall* find it together!' Drawing her sword, she raised it to the ceiling, bringing down a shower of plaster.

The power of her enthusiasm was impossible to resist. A smile spread across Alfie's face, quickly becoming a grin. 'Yes,' he said. 'Yes. We *shall* find it!'

'Excellent,' the Professor chipped in, clapping his hands together. 'Shall we be off then?'

'Hold on a second,' interrupted Prince Herkleton. 'These people *still* haven't got any money, dear. Remember?'

'Hush, my own sweet darling,' said Sir Brenda, reaching up to ruffle his hair. 'You heard what the boy said. They'll find a way to pay. Now, first we feast and sing. Herkleton, fetch ale and pickled eggs while we raise our voices in sad songs of ages past. Who wants to start?' Sir Brenda looked around. Her eyes settled on Alfie. 'You. You start.'

Alfie didn't have the heart to tell her he didn't know any sad songs of ages past. The DJs on the radio station his mum listened to never played any.

He wasn't going to let Sir Brenda down though. He *did* know all the words to the current Number One. Taking a deep breath, he lifted his voice and began to sing, 'Ooooo baby, yeah yeah baby. Oooo baby baby yeah.'

CHAPTER FIFTEEN

GUILTY LOVE FOR JAMIE FRINGE

The singing soon moved into the back room where the Professor and Sir Brenda waved foaming mugs of beer while Alfie and Derek helped themselves to a jar of pickled eggs. With each mug of beer, the singing grew louder until darkness fell and passers-by on the street outside began joining in. Hooded, giggling, and shushing everyone loudly, Sir Brenda was about to steal away into the night when Prince Herkleton dragged her back inside. Insisting the questers set off in the morning, he pointed Alfie, Derek, and the Professor to the stable and threw a pile of old blankets at them.

Alfie snuggled into warm straw feeling happier than he had since arriving on Outlandish. With Sir Brenda on Team Unusual Cartography Club the chances of success looked much better. Also, the stable was warmer and far less flea-infested than The Dead Crow. Every so often, the horse—who was called Thunderhoof—licked his face, too. Which was nice. Laying back, he wondered what his mum was doing at far end of the universe while he watched spiders go about their web-weaving business by the light of a dribbly candle.

After a while, Derek's hand reached out and turned the handle of the tiny gramophone on his chest. 'The song you sang. What was it called?' she asked. The Child of Skingrath propped herself up on an elbow, watching him. Her dark eyes glinted in the candlelight.

'*Yeah Baby,*' Alfie told her. 'It's by a singer called Jamie Fringe. Did you like it?'

'The Children of Skingrath chant of pain and sacrifice,' Derek answered slowly. 'My favourite is *O Skingrath Pull My Legs Off*. This *Yeah Baby* is stupid and pointless.'

'Yes,' Alfie agreed. 'It really is. Fun though. Have you *ever* had fun Derek? You know—fun? Enjoying yourself just because it's good to be alive?'

'Fun is useless. Life is suffering. It prepares us for Skingrath's reward: eternal torment in His Land of Fire.'

'So Skingrath *wants* you to be miserable?'

'Yes. And now he will punish me. He sees our thoughts. He knows that when you sang I wanted to . . . to . . .' Derek's face crumpled. 'To shake my bottom down,' she sobbed.

Of all the strange moments that Alfie had had since arriving at Number Four, Wigless Square, this was the fifth or sixth strangest. He stared at Derek, and—for an instant—saw a girl beneath the layers of war paint and muck. 'It seems to me,' he said, quietly, 'that any god who won't let you dance is a god who isn't worth following.'

'You are a puny idiot with strange knees. What would you know about *anything*?' Derek asked.

'I know dancing isn't wrong,' Alfie shrugged. 'Jokes are good, too. Hey, pull my finger.'

Derek ignored Alfie's finger, which was a shame

because he would have loved to introduce her to the joy and wonder of fart gags. 'You seek to tempt me away from Skingrath with your *fun*,' she hissed. 'But you will see. When we find my god he will punish you.'

'Um . . . First, I'm not going looking for Skingrath with you. As soon as we find a stone circle you're on your own. Second, how exactly is Skingrath's reward different from Skingrath's punishment? Only his Land of Fire sounds fairly horrible, too.'

'Pain is better than *fun*,' Derek hissed.

'Do you even hear yourself?' said Alfie.

'Suffering is good for the soul.'

'*Dancing* is good for the soul,' Alfie insisted.

'I *hate* you,' Derek replied. 'I hate the Wanja-faced old man, and I hate this stupid warrior with her stupid red hair, too.' Rolling over, she wrapped herself in her blanket and refused to speak again.

Alfie lay back picking woodlice out of his hair and humming *Yeah Baby*, just to annoy her.

After what seemed like only two or three hours, because it *was* only two or three hours, Sir Brenda threw the stable door open. 'Good morrow to thee, fellow questers,' she bellowed. 'Our adventure awaits.'

'But it's still dark,' Alfie groaned, pulling the blanket over his face.

'Best time. We'll miss the traffic,' replied Sir Brenda. 'Come on, Herkleton's got porridge on.'

'Is he really a prince?' Alfie yawned, sitting up and stretching.

'Oh yes,' said Sir Brenda. 'I won his hand in marriage during my first quest.'

'And he was all right about it, was he? Being given away as a prize, I mean.'

'It was very romantic,' Sir Brenda nodded. 'Moonlit balconies and kisses stolen in the rose garden and suchlike. We were terribly in love at the time. Still are, aren't we, my heart?'

'Only when you're not being a complete idiot,' said Herkleton as he entered the stable with three bowls of steaming porridge on a tray. Laying it down on an upturned barrel, he kissed his wife's cheek and pulled a piece of paper from his pocket. 'The young man said he'd find a way to pay us, so I made up your first bill,' he said, handing it to the

Professor.

The Professor took one look at it and squawked, 'Oh my Skingrath.'

SIR BRENDA'S VALIANT QUESTS

INVOICE

1. Quest advice and general plotting
   3 Gold Shillings

2. Standard feasting and singing package
   6 Gold Shillings

3. Beds for three and stabling for one magical metal horse thing
   4 Gold Shillings

4. Breakfast and wishing questers luck as they depart on their valiant journey
   3 Gold Shillings

5. Minimum one week questing time with Sir Brenda
   35 Gold Shillings

5. Handling fee
   2 Gold Shillings

TOTAL 53 Gold Shillings

By the time the breakfast was over and the
Professor and Prince Herkleton had argued over the
bill, the sun was up. Then there were six children
for Sir Brenda to kiss; questions about how many
clean vests she had packed; adjustments to be
made to the Professor's corset; promises to return
loaded with gold; saggy-backed Thunderhoof to
be saddled; and another round of farewell kisses.
Throughout, Derek refused to look at Alfie.
Standing apart, she folded her arms and tapped
a foot, growling angrily at every hug.

Finally, Alfie climbed on board Betsy.
With an explosive backfire, the moped rattled
along the cobbles behind Thunderhoof with
Derek moping at the rear. Prince Herkleton
gave them a send-off that really was good
value for money. Standing on tiptoe
and waving a handkerchief from
the shop's front step,
he cried, 'Fare thee
well, brave adventurers.
Sir Brenda's Valiant Quests
thanks you for speedy

payment and accepts no
responsibility for any deaths
that may result from
your quest.'

CHAPTER SIXTEEN
THE OPPRESSOR'S PALACE

'Um . . . where are we going?' Alfie shouted ahead.
With all the singing and feasting the night before,
The Circle of the Circle hadn't made an actual plan.

Sir Brenda looked back. 'First stop, the palace,'
she yelled. 'It has a library and the wizard there is
said to be neck-deep in forbidden knowledge. If
anyone can tell us where another circle lies, it is he.'

'Wowzers,' said Alfie, who'd been hoping for
a tour of the palace. Meeting a wizard would be
a nice bonus, too. He peered up at the skyline-
hogging building as Sir Brenda led them closer.
Spires and towers decorated with ugly gargoyles
rose above Verminium. Rings of massive stone

walls protected it. They hadn't worked against the dragon though. Half the towers were broken, stubby, and fire-blackened. Snatching his notebook from his pocket, Alfie tried to knock off a quick sketch, wishing—not for the first time—that he had brought a camera. Due to Betsy bouncing over cobbles, his picture looked like a shark having a bad hair day. He decided to have another go when they had stopped for the night. People on Earth would love a look at the Palace of Verminium.

Why shouldn't they get one?

The thought jolted Alfie upright. Why indeed? People paid a lot of money for holidays to far-off lands. Why not offer them tours of a place that was literally out of their world? And why stop at Outlandish? Quickly, he jotted the words 'Unusual Travel Agency' in his notebook, and then immediately forgot about them when Sir Brenda yelled, 'Here we are then.'

Pocketing the notebook, Alfie looked up. Ahead lay a drawbridge that crossed a wide moat. At the far end were heavy gates, barred with iron. Above them a soldier leaned on battlements, picking his nose. 'Erm . . . how do we get in?' Alfie asked.

'The sewers,' Sir Brenda whispered, pointing at a pipe that dripped brown gunge into the moat. 'We'll swim beneath the drawbridge, climb in, and sneak into the palace through the drains. Then we'll use secret passages to get to the library.'

'It doesn't sound very hygienic, Sir Brenda,' said the Professor. 'Couldn't we just . . . ah . . . knock?'

'Feeble,' spat Derek. Without bothering to remove her filthy skins, she stepped into the moat where a friendly poo nudged her ankle.

'No, seriously Derek, wait,' said Alfie. 'I think we should try knocking first.'

'By the seven-buttocked lord of chaos, no,' said Sir Brenda. 'Whoever heard of questers knocking at a castle door? No, we do this properly and that means sneaking in through the sewers, strangling rats with our bare hands as we go.'

'Are you sure?' said Alfie, gazing at the dripping pipe with disgust.

'There's also the fact that the Oppressor thinks I'm off battling goblins,' said Sir Brenda, sounding uncomfortable. 'If we knock he'll know I'm here and he's not a very nice person.'

'Yoo hoo, is that you, Sir Brenda?' cried a voice Alfie recognized. Shading his eyes, he looked up and saw Sergeant Pillage leaning over the battlements.

'Drat,' muttered the knight, shrinking as far down as possible into Thunderhoof's saddle.

It was too late. 'Hurrah, it *is* you!' the sergeant yelled. 'Back from vanquishing goblins at last! And you brought some . . . very . . . odd . . . companions. Still, I suppose any companions are better than no companions. Well done. Lord Spittelgrad *will* be pleased.'

'Oh hello, Pillage,' Sir Brenda shouted up. 'We're just here to . . .'

'No need to explain, Sir B,' the sergeant chuckled. 'I *know* why you're here. The call of wild adventure, eh? Dreadful terror and certain death. Sets the blood a-fizzing, doesn't it? Come in, come in.' The sergeant nudged the soldier next to him, accidentally setting off his crossbow.

The bolt pinged off Sir Brenda's armour.

'Clumsy oaf,' the sergeant bawled at the unfortunate soldier as he cuffed him round the back of the head. 'Report to the palace torturer for a session with the grundlespoon. No, not *now*. Open the gate for Sir Brenda and her merry band of misfits *first*, you idiot. Don't keep Outlandish's greatest hero waiting.'

Stamping feet echoed through the vast palace. Surrounded by guards, Alfie, the Professor, Derek, and Sir Brenda were led down stone corridors, almost, but not quite, like they were prisoners. A hint of 'don't try to escape' flickered in the guards' grins, and a spear's pointy end prodded Alfie's back when he stopped to look at a statue of Queen Clovis the Iron-Footed kicking Bishop Wimsley up the backside.

Eventually—with a final, palace-shaking, stamp—the guards came to a halt in an enormous chamber lined with stained-glass windows. Alfie stumbled into the Professor's back, his eyes glued to the painted ceiling.

'At last, heroes have come forth to rid Verminium of this dragon plague,' a voice creaked.

Alfie tore his eyes from the ceiling to find himself standing before a pair of thrones. On the smaller of the two sat a woman Alfie thought must be the almost lovely Daphne. 'Almost lovely', he decided, was probably not the best way to describe her. 'Almost dead' might have been better. Her head lolled like a wrinkled balloon three days after a party. A pile of knitting lay untouched in her lap. The only sign that she was alive was the fact that her moustache fluttered with her breathing. Beside her sat a man so old and withered and ugly he made the Professor look like the kind of male models you see in aftershave adverts. Dribble leaked from the corner of his mouth. Eyes, half-hidden by heavy lids, peered at the travellers like angry oysters. Lord Spittelgrad, the Oppressor of Verminium, wore robes of darkest purple and leaned forward from his throne, knobbly hands resting on a jewel-topped cane.

DISCOVERING . . . THE PALACE OF VERMINIUM

Visitors to Verminium's palace will be captivated by this grand castle, and possibly by one of the forgotten traps set up by King Spamface the Suspicious, many of which still wait to surprise people in dusty corridors. Must-see parts of the palace include . . .

THE THRONE ROOM

One of the wonders of Outlandish, the palace throne room features the famous ceiling painting of King Vermin stealing wallets from the gods by the great artist, Marcel Anglepoise.

THE DUNGEONS

Some of Verminium's most famous criminals have been tortured here and parts of them are still stuck to the walls or on spikes in the dungeon's museum.

THE LIBRARY

The palace library is reported to hold the largest collection of books in Outlandish. It has sixteen of them, including a terrifying work known as the *Textbookius Demonicus* and a copy of *Mister Tiddly Loses a Sock*, signed by the author.

QUEEN DAISY'S BEDROOM

Here you can still read the old queen's diary. Between the pages of this huge book can be found love poems written in Daisy's own hand, along with pressed flowers and the pressed hearts of the boyfriends she grew bored of.

'I said, *at last heroes have come forth*,'
the Oppressor repeated, tapping his cane
on the stone floor, impatiently. 'For too
long this terrible dragon has threatened
Verminium, demanding our riches and
burning our homes. Now, the mighty
Sir Brenda and her band of . . . of . . .'
Lord Spittelgrad leaned further forward,
peering from Alfie to the Professor to
Derek '. . . and her band of oddballs,
will slay the dreadful beast.'

'Ah,' said Sir Brenda. 'No can do, I'm afraid. I've already got a quest, you see.'

'Yes, Sir Brenda, I know,' crooned the Oppressor. '*My* quest. You shall slay the dragon and return to me . . . I mean to the *city* . . . all the treasure it has taken.'

'No, I won't.'

The Oppressor ignored her. 'And earn yourself a mountain of gold, which may contain traces of *real* gold, and not forgetting the greatest prize of all—the hand of my daughter, Daphne, in marriage.'

Hearing her name, Daphne sat up. 'Oooo lovely. I'll just get into my support stockings . . .' she said, before falling asleep again.

'Sorry, but I'm already married. The answer's still no,' Sir Brenda said, with a slight shudder.

'What's that you say, Sir Brenda?' said the Oppressor leaning forward and cupping his ear again. 'My hearing's not what it was. Please throw me and these other . . . peculiar . . . adventurers into your deepest, darkest dungeon, Lord Spittelgrad? Was *that* what you said?'

'Enough of this rudeness,' the Professor interrupted.

The Oppressor sniffed. 'Eh?' he said, fixing the Professor with a look that promised a lengthy grundlespoon experience. 'Who are *you*?'

'Professor Pewsley Bowell-Mouvemont,' the Professor snapped back, his moustache bristling. 'I happen to be the leader of this expedition and I've already hired Sir Brenda for *our* quest, so your silly dragon-slaying business will just have to wait.'

'Excuse me, could I have a quiet word,' Alfie squeaked, tugging the Professor's sleeve urgently. It was time to step in before the old man landed them all in a torture chamber.

'What is it, Rupert?' the Professor huffed. 'I'm busy.'

Alfie gave the Professor a wink. In a whisper he said, 'Tell him we'll slay the dragon but we'll need to look at the maps in the library.'

'Why would I do that?' hissed the Professor. 'He's a dreadful bully, and he *sniffed* at me. The family honour is at stake. People can't just go around sniffing at Bowell-Mouvemonts.'

'Because maps, Professor,' Alfie whispered back. '*Maps*!'

Understanding dawned on the Professor's face. '*Cunning*,' he chuckled. 'Once we've had a look at his maps we'll ignore the dragon and go straight to the stone circle. This awful fellow will never find us on the other side of the universe, eh?'

'Ssssssh,' said Alfie, nodding.

'Good job, Rupert,' said the Professor with an enormous wink. 'You're really quite a brainbox, aren't you?'

'Thanks,' whispered Alfie, who *was* feeling quite proud of himself.

The Professor straightened up and turned back to the Oppressor. 'Sorry about that,' he said. 'My young friend here has reminded me that slaying the dragon is *exactly* the quest we're looking for. We will, of course, need to take a look at the maps in your library.'

'I can spare you the walk,' croaked the Oppressor. 'I've already summoned Geeseparty, the librarian and . . . oh, here he comes now.'

A young man carrying a scroll the size of a small rug stumbled across the floor, tripping over the hem of his own robes. Alfie was disappointed.

The wizard didn't even have a pointy hat. He was young, beardless, and spotty.

'Good morning, my lord,' said Geeseparty. 'We will be needing a table, I think.'

Lord Spittelgrad raised a finger. Servants rushed forward carrying a table and set it in front of the Oppressor.

'There,' said Geeseparty rolling out his map.

Alfie leaned over. The Professor's head appeared over one shoulder; Sir Brenda's over the other. 'I *say*, that's a very good map,' squawked the Professor. 'I've seen a few in my time and this one's a beauty, Mr Mousetart.'

'Geeseparty,' said Geeseparty. '*Doctor* Geeseparty.'

'Quite so, Mr Mousetart. Quite so,' muttered the Professor.

'Geeseparty,' said Geeseparty.

Alfie wasn't listening. He was too busy staring at the map. It was *exactly* what they had been looking for. The map was twenty times the size of the map of Outlandish in *The Cosmic Atlas*, and much more detailed. Alfie squinted, eyes searching for any sign of a stone circle. Parts of the map were *moving*. Small fluffy clouds drifted across the landscape. Tiny waterfalls gushed blue ink. 'It's *magical*,' he breathed.

'Yes, well, *hello*: wizard,' said Geeseparty. 'Master of the dark arts and all that. Now, to get to the dragon's lair you'll follow the same road as the carts of gold we have to send. As you can see the dragon has nested . . .'

'In this cave,' yelped Alfie, jabbing a finger. 'Which also contains a stone circle.'

'Brilliant,' cried the Professor. 'Good old Mousetart. The day is saved!'

Even Derek seemed excited for once. 'Skingrath,' she whispered. Stepping closer, she gazed at the spot where Alfie was still pointing. To the north of Verminium, beyond the great stretch of Hinderwood, rose Mount Gallyvant. Curled around the mountain's peak was a dragon. Inside the mountain was cave. In the centre of the cave was a stone circle, drawn the size of an ant's hat.

'Oh yes,' said Geeseparty, peering at the map. 'I hadn't noticed that. Well, well, well . . . A stone circle, eh? How odd. Umm, remind me why we care.'

'We don't,' croaked the Oppressor, tapping his cane once again. 'What we care about is the gold. Remember, I want *all* the treasure back. I shall be *very* disappointed if any of it accidentally falls into someone's pocket, though I'm sure the palace torturer would be happy to take it out again, along with a lot of teeth and a few important bones.'

'Obviously, the dragon won't allow you anywhere near its hoard of treasure,' Geeseparty cut in, 'so you'll have to make sure it's properly dead first.'

In his excitement at finding a way back to his mum, Alfie had overlooked the dragon. 'About that,' he said. 'As a wizard, do you happen to have anything that might help with the dragon-slaying side of things? A magic sword or something?'

'Oh yes,' said the wizard, patting his robe. 'I've got a Slay-o-Matic Magical Dragon Exterminator about my person somewhere. Kills one hundred percent of all dragons, you know.'

'*Really?*' said Alfie, brightening up.

'No, not really,' said the wizard. He stopped patting himself. 'There is no known way to slay a dragon. That's why everyone who has ever tried is now dead. Do you see?'

CHAPTER SEVENTEEN
THREE HUNDRED MILES IN ONE CHAPTER

Leaving the bright lights and smoking patches of Verminium behind, the band of questers raced across Outlandish at speeds of between seven and nine-and-a-half miles per hour, according to Betsy's speed-o-meter. Every so often, the Professor made everyone stop so he could check the information in *The Cosmic Atlas*. Alfie helped, and soon became expert with the old brass instruments the Professor used for measuring the landscape. He also learned a lot more about the UCC, stone circles, and other worlds. The Professor loved to chatter while Betsy bounced across Outlandish, and his favourite subject was the Unusual Cartography Club. A typical conversation went something like this . . .

'So you see, young Rupert, during the Great Exploration Period humans found lots of worlds. There are probably *thousands* of old stone circles dotted around the universe, but most are lost now. We only have the coordinates for a few hundred noted in *The Cosmic Atlas*. The club has been trying to rediscover more . . .'

'Ouch! That was a really big rock. Can't you watch where you're steering?" Alfie interrupted, his bottom bouncing on Betsy's hard, leather seat. He leaned over to rummage in a saddlebag. 'I think my bum's gone purple. Did we bring any cushions? *Why* didn't we bring any cushions?'

'Oh yes, sorry. I forgot the cushions. Anyway, as I was saying: old circles on lost worlds *do* turn up from time to time. I once found the coordinates to a place called Whiff-Whiff. Someone at the UCC had scribbled them on a paper napkin and shoved it to the back of a sock drawer.

'You found a lost world at the back of a sock drawer?' Alfie asked, blinking. The Unusual Cartography club was a very strange place.

'Mmm-hmm,' the Professor replied 'I popped over, just to see what it was like, and the people there greet you by sniffing your armpits. A whole planet full of armpit sniffers! Dreadful place. No wonder everyone forgot about it. Of course, if you've got a stone circle you can go *anywhere* and the UCC is always on the lookout for brand new planets. To discover a *new* planet you have to open an Explorer's Pathway to random coordinates and hope for the best. I've discovered twelve, you know. It's a UCC record.'

'Isn't that method a bit hit-and-miss?' asked Alfie.

'You *do* spend quite a lot of time walking through the circle into empty space with a rope tied around your waist,' the Professor replied. 'So you can pull yourself back, see? Also, it's cold: space. Always wear extra underwear. That's what I do.'

'I see,' said Alfie. 'Oh no, a ditch. *There*. Watch out, Professor! Watch . . . *ahhhhhhhh.*'

CRASH

'Oh dear, are you all right Rupert?' asked the Professor a few minutes later when the dust had settled.

At which point Sir Brenda trotted past on Thunderhoof. 'Come on you two,' she said. 'No time for laying around in ditches. There's a long way to go yet.'

Every evening Alfie sat at the campfire trying not to think about the minutes and hours slowly trickling by on Earth. To pass the time, he chatted to Sir Brenda about the sights of Outlandish or to the Professor about other strange worlds the old man had visited.

Every morning Alfie wound the gramophone around his neck and tried to ignore his aching bottom when he and the Professor climbed aboard Betsy. He didn't need the translator often though. Only the Professor talked. Derek just grunted now and then while Sir Brenda rode quietly as they journeyed through villages with exotic names like Grumblehog and Leaky Pigeon. Alfie watched her, worried. Sir Brenda was Outlandish's greatest hero but she often bit her bottom lip, staring ahead with a frown on her face. She was worried, Alfie knew. A deadly destiny lay ahead: a battle with the dragon.

How were they going to kill it? Alfie, who was beginning to realize that he had a talent for solving problems, was stumped. Putting it to the back of his mind, he took measurements with the Professor and filled his notepad with details of the places they passed through. As it will save a lot of travelling time, let's take a peek at some of the entries . . .

DISCOVERING . . . EEEVILLE

With its magnificent graveyards and ruined castles, Eeeville is a place where history comes alive—very much like its dead. The town has a busy nightlife for those who enjoy running about waving a flaming torch or pitchfork. Indeed, the locals have a favourite saying: 'If you can't have a good time in Eeeville you're aaaaarggggh . . . it's got my foot. Get it off. Get IT OFFFF . . .'

WHERE TO STAY

Castle Eeeeq ★★★★★

Castle Eeeeq offers FREE five-star accommodation to 'weary travellers'. Here, you can relax by a roaring fire while hunchbacked servants attend to your every need. Later, you can explore the castle while running screaming through its maze of corridors.

JOIN US FOR THE CASTLE EEEEQ MURDER MYSTERY WEEKEND

Who will murder you first? The bald giant, the square-headed lurching thug, the twins of evil, or The Marrrrrster?

It's a mystery!

Blood Drip Inn ★★★

Boasting that up to forty percent of its customers survive the night, the Blood Drip Inn provides its guests with a gift basket in every room. This contains wooden stakes, garlic necklaces, and silver daggers. The beds all have extra-thick duvets, giving guests something to chew on when ghastly faces look in at the window.

WHERE TO EAT

The Garlic Patch ***
Garlic is central to the town's cuisine, and The
Garlic Patch restaurant offers an exciting range
of garlic breads, garlic soups, and garlic trifle, all
of which add to the town's general stench.

Rock Coffin **
Big hair and ritual sacrifice are all the rage at
Rock Coffin where local bands including The Gas-
Powered Toads, Graverobber Sweetheart, and Demon
Toenails wail classic hits such as 'Ahh, We're all
Going to Die!' while biting the heads off small
creatures. Bar snacks are available, but are to be
avoided.

DISCOVERING . . . FAIRY DELL
The delightfully named Fairy Dell, with its
wildflowers and pretty waterfall, does not
contain any fairies. It does contain swarms
of angry tortoises.

DISCOVERING . . .
THE WANDERING FAIR

As its name suggests, the merchants, entertainers, and thieves of Outlandish's Wandering Fair travel across the country. Fair days are always a great event for locals, with many nailing their doors and windows shut and hiding under their beds. Those lucky enough to visit the fair will find stalls selling every kind of stolen and fake magical goods as well as jugglers, fire-breathers, acrobats, and fortune tellers who can tell you exactly when you will be robbed—usually by the jugglers, fire-breathers, acrobats, and fortune tellers.

ROLL UP FOR THE TRAVELLING FAIR'S CHILDREN'S CIRCUS!

★ Our contortionist has his legs stuck behind his ears!

★ Prod him with a stick if you like—there's nothing he can do about it!

★ Mister Giggles steals your jewellery!

★ PLUS . . . Egbert the Tattooed Chicken! Dancing Broccoli! Boring Puppets!

DISCOVERING . . . GLURPMIRE

This small village of mouldy huts falling into a bog is the place to be for mosquito fans. Here you'll meet some of the most depressed people ever to sob into their hands, while soaking up the views of thick fog. Attractions include the Glurpmire Bog Man, a well-preserved ancient body which was dragged out of the bog after thousands of years. He now offers travellers mudbaths and head massages.

WHERE TO STAY

The Hummock *

A dismal wet hill, The Hummock offers a place to pitch a tent where travellers might not get sucked into the bog or eaten by alligators overnight. Be prepared to share your accommodation with Glurpmire's vast clouds of biting insects.

WHERE TO EAT

The Mudshack *

The famous Mudshack restaurant features a large tank of brown water, containing eels. Customers can choose their own. The chef will beat it to death and then fry it at the table.

And so, our valiant questers came to Hinderwood. The forest stretched across the whole of Outlandish—a thick line of black and green, separating the north of the country from the south and separating the travellers from their destiny. One road, and one road only, passed through it—a pathway dark with danger. Despair oozed from the shadows between the trees, sending goosebumps up Alfie's spine as he packed up camp.

In the deep, dark woods things waited.

Alfie knew things waited because the Professor and Sir Brenda were sat by the fire, drinking tea, and staring at Doctor Geeseparty's magical map. Occasionally, one of them rubbed their chin and tapped a finger on the parchment, pointing to one of Hinderwood's waiting things . . .

As far as Alfie could see the only thing that wasn't waiting for them in Hinderwood was a nice picnic area. 'Don't suppose you'd like to give me a hand, would you?' he asked Derek, as he staggered past her with his arms full of tent.

The Child of Skingrath was sitting on a rock, sharpening her dagger. 'No,' she said.

Alfie's nose wrinkled. Derek's rabbit-skin clothes were getting proper whiffy. Paint and mud peeled from her face, making it look like she'd been badly wallpapered. He decided not to mention it. He hadn't had a shower or changed his underwear in over a week and was getting a bit stinky, too. Instead, he asked, 'How about keeping me company? Could you manage that at least?'

Derek grunted.

'Aw, come on. You haven't spoken to anyone in days,' he continued. 'This journey would be much more fun if you smiled once in a while.'

'You know my feelings about fun,' Derek replied. 'I'm against it.'

'Come on, just one smile.'

'You are frightened,' said Derek. 'That is why

you babble at me like the rear end of a Cabbage-Eating Fartpig. It is embarrassing to see your pathetic fear.'

'Doesn't the dragon scare *you*?'

Derek looked up, a sneer cracking her layers of paint. 'Fear is for weaklings, like you. Take your gutless babbling somewhere else.'

'I'm just trying to be friendly.'

'*Friendly*. Prrrrrp.' Derek blew a sound that Alfie decided must be an impression of the Fartpig.

'Mature,' he muttered. 'Really mature.'

'Prrrrrrp,' Derek repeated. 'Fartpig, you understand? I am making the noise of a Cabbage-Eating Fartpig's rear end, because that is what you sound like.'

'Yes,' Alfie snapped. 'And you're having *fun* with it, I can tell.'

'Not fun,' Derek replied. 'I feel a warrior's fierce joy when vanquishing an unworthy foe.'

'But you're smiling. So, ask yourself: who's *really* won here?'

The smile disappeared from Derek's face. 'You think you are clever,' she growled. 'So think about this: your weakness means our quest will fail. You will never see your precious *mum* again, but whether we live or die *I* shall find Skingrath.'

'*I* am not afraid,' the Skingrathian girl continued. 'So who wins now?' Testing the edge of her dagger with a thumb, she watched blood run down her wrist.

Alfie bit down on the snappy reply he had lined up. Derek was right. The quest was doomed. None of them had come up with a plan to kill the dragon and they had barely enough weapons to battle a sleepy hedgehog. 'You're right,' he said, quietly, 'I *am* scared. I thought talking might help, but I guess I picked the wrong person. Sorry to have bothered you.' Turning, he walked away.

'Pitiful coward,' Derek called after him.

Alfie carried on walking. He might never see his mum again, but he had no choice but to try. In the meantime, there was the breakfast table to fold up, candlesticks to polish, and the Professor's flower arrangement to empty from its vase. He strapped on his crash helmet, trembling as he took his seat on Betsy, and peered over the Professor's shoulder into the depths of Hinderwood.

Sir Brenda mounted Thunderhoof. The horse snickered nervously, eying the forest ahead. Sir Brenda patted her mount and turned in the saddle. 'Listen up, noble questers,' she said. 'Fearful danger lurks in yonder woodland. This is intermediate-to-advanced-level questing. I want everyone to stick together. No matter what happens *no one* leaves the path. Yes, that means you, too, young lady. Understand?'

Derek glared, but nodded.

Alfie nodded too. He didn't trust his voice not to come out as a frightened squeak.

The Professor snapped his goggles into place and kick-started Betsy. 'Bowell-Mouvement ready to go,' he bellowed.

'Good,' said Sir Brenda. 'As we ride, I will teach you how to deal with some of the terrors we may face.'

Clumped together, the four questers cantered, motored, and ran towards the forest until Alfie could see a small break in the cliff-face of tangled trees—a narrow path so overgrown it looked more like a tunnel than a road. Wind tossed Hinderwood's branches. Hissing leaves threatened anyone who dared enter. Gloom closed in around them. Twigs stretched out to grab his hair and scratch his face. Knotted tree trunks formed hideous, leering faces. Somewhere, deep in the forest, something chuckled.

'First, giant poisonous spiders,' said Sir Brenda. 'If you see a giant poisonous spider coming at you your best friend is a magical blade. Does anyone have a magical blade?'

'No,' Alfie squeaked.

'Hmmm,' said Sir Brenda. 'Then the best way to deal with a giant poisonous spider is by running away screaming and flapping your arms.'

CHAPTER EIGHTEEN

THE HORRORS OF HINDERWOOD

'Werewolves,' continued Sir Brenda. 'The best way to deal with a werewolf is to go full woodchopper. Of course, *we* forgot to bring an axe so I would suggest . . .'

'Running away, screaming, and flapping our arms?' Alfie cut in, gloomily.

'Excellent,' said Sir Brenda. 'You're getting it now. And that brings us to witches. If you see a witch coming at you . . .'

The Professor put up a hand, making Betsy wobble dangerously. 'Ah, I know this one. You cut a wart off and let the air out,' he said. 'Witches are inflatable. Like lilos. Isn't that right, Sir Brenda?'

'I wish it were,' said Sir Brenda. 'Because an inflatable witch would not be a difficult foe to vanquish. You could burst one with a pin or, indeed, cut a wart off and watch her whizz around the place while slowly deflating. Sadly, however, I have never met a blow-up witch.'

'Are you sure?' said the Professor. 'I'm sure I read somewhere that they're inflatable.'

'Witches are *not* inflatable,' continued Sir Brenda, firmly. 'But they are *inflammable*. The best course of action with witches is burning them. Dropping a house on them gives good results, too. Or you could just . . .'

'Run away, screaming, and flapping your arms?' Alfie repeated automatically while staring into the green depths of Hinderwood. The forest's murmurs teased him with rustles and creaks, almost as if the trees were trying to speak.

'*Exactly.*' Sir Brenda nodded. 'You're terrific questing material young fellow, I must say. You'd do well in the job.'

'Really?' said Alfie, snapping his attention back to the knight. 'I always thought questing was more about fighting enemies and less about running away from them, flapping your arms, and screaming.'

'Lots of people think that,' said the knight. 'And lots of people die. Always pick your battles, young fellow, and never pick one you can't win. Besides, screaming and flapping your arms makes the enemy think you're scared. So they won't be expecting it when you sneak up behind them, this time equipped with a magical blade, axe, box of matches, or house. Then, *bosh*—another quest successfully completed and back home to marry the prince. Or—if you've already married the prince—a hot dinner and a cuddle.'

'So, if it's magic swords for spiders, axes for werewolves, and fire or houses for witches, what do we need to kill a dragon?' Alfie blurted, regretting it instantly. He already knew Sir Brenda had no idea.

An uncomfortable silence settled. Sir Brenda scowled while Thunderhoof plodded on. 'Where was I?' she said after a few minutes. 'Oh yes: what to do if you're attacked by an *elf*.'

Alfie's ears pricked up—which was quite fitting, considering. '*Elves*,' he gasped. 'There are *elves* in Outlandish?'

'In actual fact, there are elves on a lot of worlds,' the Professor interrupted. 'They're very pretty but a completely different species from humans, of course. A bit like a nasty rash though. Painful and difficult to get rid of. How they get around is one of those mysteries. No one really likes to ask them. Mainly because no one really likes getting a poke in the eye.'

'Are there elves on Earth?' Alfie demanded.

The Professor shrugged. 'Never seen one,' he said with a shudder. 'Thank goodness.'

'There may not be elves in your world but there are elves in *Hinderwood*,' said Sir Brenda. She looked around. 'Probably watching us now; nasty, pointy-eared little beggars.'

'But elves are *good*,' said Alfie.

'Good at shooting you in the back from behind a tree,' Sir Brenda replied.

'They're on *our* side,' Alfie insisted. 'I've read that in books.'

Sir Brenda turned in the saddle to stare at Alfie. 'Elves are on *elves*' side,' she said, grimly. 'Don't think they're *nice* just because they have swishy hair, and whatever you do, do *not* let them lure you into the woods.'

The path wound on into forest darkness. Alfie slipped back into a silence, slumped against the baggage, and stared into the trees. Wind whispered through the leaves, weaving sly forest magic.

A quick note of explanation is needed here. While wind whispering through leaves may not sound very magical, it is—in fact—a very difficult and delicate branch of magic known as 'murmurancy'. Elves are really good at it. As the hours passed, Alfie's fear dwindled. It seemed that the trees murmured his name over and over again. Strangely, Alfie didn't find this spooky. Slowly, he relaxed. The forest was a wild place, the trees told him, but all the more wonderful for being untamed. How could it *not* be wonderful when it was the home of elves?

Elves *were* good, Alfie was

sure. Elves were cool and

magical and . . .

'Rupert, be a good

lad and put the tent up

would you?'

Jolted out of his

daydream, Alfie found it

had become a nightdream.

Hours had passed. Above his

head, Outlandish's twin moons

were chopped into a jigsaw by

branches. The forest rustled, sighed,

scrabbled, and chittered around him but

the Professor's voice had broken the

spell. The murmurs had gone.

'No tents,' announced Sir Brenda,

peering into the dark and pulling her sword.

'No fires either. We'll take turns at keeping

watch, and move on at first light.'

'No fire,' spluttered the Professor.

'But that means no tea! I *must*

have a cup of tea.'

'Not tonight, old man,' said
the knight, clapping the
Professor on the shoulder.
'We don't want to attract
attention.'

'I will hunt rabbit,' Derek
interrupted, unexpectedly.
'We should eat.'

'No fires,' Sir Brenda
repeated. 'No tea. No cooking.'

Derek shot her a withering
look. 'Who said anything about
cooking?' she said. 'Raw flesh is good.
The blood reminds us of the blood of
our enemies. The bones remind us to
give thanks to Skingrath who gave us bones
so that we would not flop over to one side
when fighting our enemies.'

Shaking off the forest's magical fog, Alfie
said, 'Why did Skingrath give *rabbits* bones
then? Do rabbits have enemies?'

'Yes,' Derek spat. 'Me.'

'Stop bickering, the pair of you,' snapped Sir Brenda. 'Something might hear. No hunting, and absolutely no leaving the path.'

'I'll take the first watch,' said Alfie. The forest was murmuring to him again, faintly, and he really, really wanted to listen. It told him there was nothing to be afraid of; that everything was going to work out just fine.

For a moment, Alfie thought about telling Sir Brenda about the whispers, but the murmuring forest told him not to. Alfie nodded to himself. The secret whispers were his, and his alone, to hear. This was a shame because if Alfie *had* said something, Sir Brenda wouldn't have let him take first watch. Or any watch at all. No, she would have tied Alfie up and made everyone sit on him all night. Because the whispering murmurancy was the first sign that the elves were coming for you, and when the elves came for you they only ever had one thing in mind: to mess you up real bad.

TRAVEL WARNING . . . HINDERWOOD

Travellers say that on the east coast of southern Outlandish is the seaport of Wrecks-Gruesome, which offers a ferry service to the port of Balingwater in northern Outlandish. This route means that Hinderwood can be avoided completely. Both seaports are cut-throat places infested by pirates, drunken sailors, and sea hags. The sea journey itself is a nightmare. If you're not throwing up over the side, you'll be screaming in terror as your leaky ship skims past giant whirlpools or is reduced to matchsticks by enraged sea monsters. It is, however, a much, much safer way to travel to northern Outlandish than through Hinderwood.

CHAPTER NINETEEN
THE RUNNING OF
THE TWONK

The elf waited until Sir Brenda, the Professor, and
Derek were asleep before it came for Alfie, and it
did have swishy hair. It fell in long, shining, just-
stepped-out-of-the-salon glossy midnight black
over the elf's shoulders, and was held back by a
silver circlet to reveal pointed ears. It—or *he*, Alfie
realized—squatted on his haunches before him in a
shaft of silvery moonlight and gazed at Alfie. From
his shoulder hung a bow carved from bone and a
quiver of arrows, fletched with the feathers of a
snowy owl. He wore sewn-together skins and a
green cloak with the careless style of someone who
could wear a cardigan knitted by their grandma and
still be the coolest person in the room.

Alfie blinked, his heart thumping. He wasn't the kind of boy who worried about clothes, but he suddenly wished his outfit wasn't from a charity shop. His trembling fingers reached for the tiny gramophone hanging around his neck and wound it tight. 'You're ... you're ... *wow*,' Alfie breathed, and then blushed. He'd only just managed to stop himself saying 'beautiful' and that would have been awkward.

The elf seemed able to read his mind. 'Yes. Beautiful. I know,' he said, his voice tinkling like a silvery brook and his emerald eyes gleaming as if he was enjoying a joke no one else would ever get. 'Are you ready, Alfie Fleet?' the elf added.

Alfie blinked. 'Ready for what?'

'Ready for the night.' Standing, the elf tipped his head towards the forest. 'Ready for the hunt.'

Alfie glanced at his sleeping companions. Compared to the elf they all looked like they'd been hit in the face with an ugly stick. He seemed to remember there was some reason he should stay with them, but he couldn't think why. It wasn't important, he was sure. This was an elf. An actual *elf*. Turning back to the beautiful creature, he said, 'Yes. I'm ready.'

'Then come.' Holding out a hand, the elf pulled Alfie to his feet. With a flick of hair, he turned and darted soundlessly into the forest.

Alfie followed, but not so silently. Twigs cracked beneath his clumsy feet as he broke into a run and left the path behind.

Behind him a pair of eyes opened.

'Hop bun Skingrath, bah skim toast,' Derek muttered to herself as she watched Alfie stumble into the darkness. 'Bunga a'dro perweegrr fishcake.' Or, in English: 'Oh my god, what a twonk. I *totally* knew he wasn't going to last five minutes.'

Alfie didn't hear, and wouldn't have cared if he had. He was running with elves—or one elf at least—through a magic forest, and he was far too busy trying to keep up. The elf flitted ahead, leaping gracefully over the same fallen logs that tripped Alfie in the darkness, dodging branches that tugged at Alfie's jumper and left his own greasy hair full of broken twigs.

'What's your name?' Alfie called ahead.

The elf looked back without breaking his stride, and shouted. Instantly translating the words, the bouncing device on Alfie's chest said, 'My name is Hoodwink. *Prince* Hoodwink. Come, Alfie Fleet. Follow.'

Alfie's trainer snagged a root. He fell to his hands and knees, panting in the darkness. The elf's name sent a shiver through him. Hoodwink, he knew, meant to cheat or trick; to mislead, trap, and deceive. He'd been expecting the creature to be called something like Eldoroliol or Runestar or Twiggin—the sort of name elves had in the books he read. For the first time, it occurred to him that Sir Brenda might have been right. Perhaps shiny, manageable hair and interesting ears didn't automatically make someone a good person. Not that the elf was even a proper person. Hoodwink might look a bit like a human being but there was something about him that was very . . . Alfie searched for a word. *Alien* was the best he could do.

Hoodwink was suddenly standing above him, holding out a hand to help him up. 'Come, Alfie Fleet. I have something to show you,' he said.

'Umm . . .' Alfie replied. He wanted to say 'no', but his mouth wouldn't form the word. He was hypnotized by the elf's glittering eyes.

'Come,' Hoodwink said again, his smile widening. 'See.'

The last of Alfie's doubts burned away on the brightness of Hoodwink's teeth. Taking the elf's hand he pulled himself up. 'Could we . . . ah . . . slow down a bit?' he asked.

'Practice running, my friend,' the elf replied with a wink. 'The hunt, remember?'

Before Alfie could reply, Hoodwink bounded away through the forest. With a groan, Alfie forced his aching legs into action, ridiculously pleased with himself. An actual elf prince had called him his *friend*.

'See,' the elf said, half an hour later.

Alfie nodded, unable to speak for two reasons. First, he was panting too hard. Second, he was totally and utterly gobsmacked. Astonished. Bewowzered. It felt like his jaw had come away from the rest of his head. The elven village was everything he'd dreamed it would be—a fantasy made real. Magical lights glowed softly in the gnarled branches of ancient trees, shining on carved treehouses. Everywhere, there were elves. Some wore crowns of leaves, others circlets of gold, and every single one of them had hair that shone. Alfie put his own hand to his head, brushing the worst of the twigs out of his own dirty mop, then let it fall again. It was useless. No matter how many times he used his mum's budget conditioner, he knew he would never have hair that good.

Staring with Frisbee-wide eyes, he struggled for breath. After a minute or so he finally managed to pant out, 'You . . . all . . . look . . . like . . . supermodels. Do . . . you . . . use . . . a . . . s-s-special shampoo?'

'Well, yes. Obviously,' Hoodwink replied, 'but we are not here to discuss haircare products.'

'Oh yeah,' Alfie panted. 'The hunt. Look, can't we just—you know—hang out? Sing sad songs of ages past or something. Only I've never hunted before and I'm pretty tired already.'

'You'll soon get the hang of it,' Hoodwink said, with a gentle smile.

Before Alfie could reply the elf lifted a silver horn and blew a note of such sweetness Alfie's face broke into a stupid grin. Across the village, heads turned. 'The forest provides fresh prey, my people,' Hoodwink called. 'Tonight we hunt.'

Turning to Alfie he added, softly, 'Are you ready, Alfie Fleet?'

Still grinning like a twerp, Alfie nodded. 'OK then,' he said. 'I'll give it a whirl.'

'Good,' said Hoodwink. 'Scar slicker tish ba-ba

snurf esclorian twa spedoolicon jelly.'

Alfie grinned. 'Sorry,' he said, winding up the translator around his neck. 'I didn't catch that last bit. What were you saying?'

'I said, we'll give you a head start of fifty heartbeats. If you make it back to your camp before we catch you we will allow you to live.'

The grin dropped from Alfie's face. *'Eh?'* he said.

'I've seen you run though,' Prince Hoodwink replied. 'You won't make it back. Forty-six heartbeats.'

'Um . . . can we just back up for a second? You're hunting *me?'* Alfie babbled.

'You are slow when you need to be quick, Alfie Fleet.' Hoodwink shrugged his bow into his hand and twanged the string. 'Yes, we are hunting you. Though it won't be much fun. You're making it too easy. Thirty-two heartbeats.'

'But I don't understand . . .' Alfie began.

'You've been Hoodwinked,' grinned the elf. 'Run, Alfie Fleet. *Run.'*

DISCOVERING . . . ELVENGLADE

The most enchanting place you could ever hope to be murdered, Hinderwood's treehouse village of Elvenglade rings to the sound of merry elvish laughter. It is worth noting that it will be YOUR pathetic struggles to escape that the elves are laughing at. Anyone with an eye for style and lucky enough to survive more than five minutes might enjoy Elvenglade's many fashion boutiques and hair salons. Visitors to The Honey Bath health spa can treat themselves to a range of beauty treatments, including the Total-Body Sandpapering and the Bee Sting Face Mask. These won't do your skin any good at all, but the elves enjoy the screaming.

CHAPTER TWENTY
WHEN ELVES ATTACK

Alfie plunged headlong into the forest. He no longer cared about his hair, or his tired muscles. He ran for his life. Branches lashed his face. Brambles snagged his legs. Tears of terror and betrayal and his own stupidity blurred his eyes. He ran, and ran, and ran, the laughter of elves ringing in his ears. Soon—too soon—it was drowned by a blast from Hoodwink's hunting horn. 'Coming, ready or not,' he heard the elf shout. More laughter followed.

Alfie plunged onwards into unfriendly darkness. He hadn't put enough distance between him and the elves: not nearly enough. And now they were gaining on him with every passing second. A root tripped him. Yelping, Alfie fell head first, with arms windmilling, down a slope, pinballing off tree trunks. With him fell an avalanche of stones and earth. Fresh tears stung his eyes.

'We *hear* you Alfie Fleet,' sang the taunting voice of Hoodwink not far behind. 'That sounded painful. *Ouches.*'

The gramophone around his neck was still translating. Alfie was tempted to tear it off and throw it into the trees, but there was no time. Ignoring his new cuts and bruises he ran again, thrashing blindly through branches.

The hunting horn sounded again. 'You are not very stealthy, Alfie Fleet.'

More elvish laughter echoed through the woods, even closer now.

Alfie staggered away from the sound, trying— and failing—to move noiselessly.

'Oh, and you're going in the wrong direction.'

A hiss escaped from between Alfie's clenched teeth. He had to *think*. Desperately, he looked around. It was too dark to see anywhere he might hide and, anyway, the elves were expert hunters. He'd be spotted in a second. He shot a look upwards. The trees were high, but once he'd climbed one there would *definitely* be no escape.

'*Think*,' he whispered to himself.

The elves wanted him to run. They wanted him to be afraid. He'd have to do something they would never expect.

Fight.

Alfie groaned. His only chance was to surprise the hunters, and the last thing the elves would be expecting was for their prey to turn round and put up a fight.

Fighting the elves didn't offer much of a chance but it was better than waiting for an arrow to hit him in the back. Slightly better. Not much better at all, really. The only good thing about fighting was that he might get to wipe the grin of Hoodwink's face before he died.

Worth it. Alfie skidded to a halt, leaves rustling beneath his feet.

'Why have you stopped, Alfie Fleet?' Hoodwink's giggling voice filtered through the trees. 'Have you given up?'

'Yes,' said Alfie, sinking to his knees and sobbing the word out. 'I'm lost, I can't run any further, and you have completely outwitted me.'

'How utterly tragic,' said Hoodwink, walking out of the shadows and flicking his hair. 'You were hardly any fun at all. Terrible prey. I hope your companions do better.'

Alfie's fingers groped in the layer of leaves on the forest floor as the elf stepped closer. 'I-I'm s-sorry I was so useless,' he wept. 'Could I please, just l-look at you for a moment b-before you kill me. You are so . . .'

'Beautiful, I know,' smiled Hoodwink. Pulling a dagger from his belt, Prince Hoodwink struck a pose in front of Alfie: hand on hip, eyes looking out into the distance as if he'd seen something ever-so-slightly sad there, and—most importantly—jutting his chin out.

Alfie's fingers found what they'd been looking for. Screaming 'Yaaaaaahhhh!' he rocketed upwards, swinging a fallen branch.

Boff. It connected with Hoodwink's chin, sending the elf staggering backwards into a tree. 'Oww,' the elf cried. 'That *really* hurt.'

'Good,' growled Alfie. He stepped forwards, raising the branch above his head.

The elf rubbed his chin and looked in horror at the muck on his own hand. 'You've made me *dirty*,' he whispered in disbelief. 'And is that *blood*? If that's blood you are in serious trouble.' A scowl crossed his perfect features. Hoodwink raised his dagger.

It was over, Alfie realized. The elf had a long, pointed, and beautifully engraved dagger. Probably magical judging by the way it glowed with a soft blue light. All he had was a stick, which, he now saw, had broken in half.

But if he was going to die then he was going to dirty the elf up a bit more first. Snarling, he raised the half-stick higher, at which point a figure stepped out from behind the tree and put a knife to Hoodwink's throat. 'To answer your question it's not blood on your chin,' the figure said. 'But the trickle you feel running down your neck right now: *that's* blood.'

The half-stick dropped from Alfie's fingers. He goggled. Then gurgled. After that he managed to choke out a few words: 'Oh,' he said. 'Hi Derek.'

Derek's eyes shone in the double moonlight.
'Hello twonk,' she said.

CHAPTER TWENTY-ONE

CHILDREN OF SKINGRATH UNDER-SIXTEENS CHAMPION

'It's nice of you to save my life,' Alfie gabbled. '*Really* nice. I mean *thanks* . . .'

'Be silent,' growled Derek. 'There are others of his kind close by.'

A smile crept over Hoodwink's face. 'Yes,' he said. 'Oh look, here they come now. Well, this was fun, but now we will just kill you *and* your smelly friend, Alfie Fleet. *Sheesh*, by the way. Is it a sweat problem, smelly friend?'

'What would you prefer to lose first?' hissed Derek, pressing her knife a little harder. 'The ears, or the hair?'

The elf paled. 'Not the hair,' he gulped. 'Don't touch the hair.'

Derek spat on the ground. 'Vain fool. I'll . . .'

'Um . . . Derek,' said Alfie.

'. . . then pull your eyeballs out and make you look up your own . . .'

'Derek,' Alfie repeated, with slightly more urgency.

'*What?*' said Derek.

'We have company,' said Alfie, looking around. More elves were looming out of the shadows. In their hands, all pointing in Derek and Alfie's direction, were arrows, spears, crossbows, swords, daggers, pikes, and a horrible-looking contraption with teeth that Alfie couldn't name.

'Oh,' said Derek. 'I may have some difficulty killing this many.'

'Not to worry,' said Alfie. 'I just remembered something.'

Turning to face the elven hunters, he cleared his throat and said, 'Good evening everyone.'

'Hiya!' called an elf near the back, waving.

'Shhh, Sparklelegs,' said another. 'We're *supposed* to be menacing.'

'Oops! Sorry.'

'As I was saying,' Alfie continued. 'You'll notice that my friend has a knife to *Prince* Hoodwink's throat. I should probably point out that she is the Children of Skingrath under-sixteens champion with that knife and also a bit bad-tempered. *Prince* Hoodwink has already managed to cheese her off, so if you value the life of your *prince* I think it would be best all round if you all dropped your weapons.'

'Don't do it,' hissed the elven prince.

In a flash, Derek took her knife from Prince Hoodwink's throat and held it to his forehead, at the roots of his hair. A couple of strands wafted to the forest floor.

'Do it,' Hoodwink wailed. 'Do it *now*.'

The elves looked from one to another. The sound of metal on dead leaves echoed around the forest as they dropped their weapons.

'Much better,' said Alfie. 'Well, this has all been very exciting but we'll be off now. Prince Hoodwink will be kindly guiding us back to our camp and staying as our guest until we leave the forest. If you don't want a bald prince then the rest of you may want to clear our path of any giant spiders, man-eating trees, vicious goblins, and whatever. But stay out of my sight. Understand?'

A murmur went round the crowd.

'Do what he says,' squealed Prince Hoodwink, who had started shaking when Alfie mentioned the word 'bald'.

'*Understand*?' Alfie said, loudly.

'Yeeeees,' chorused the elves.

'Good,' said Alfie. 'Oh, and one more thing: Sparklelegs? *Really*?'

'Yeah,' grumped the elf. 'I didn't choose it.'

As the elves trooped away, Alfie took Hoodwink's dagger, holding the glowing blade up before his eyes. At last, the questers had a magical weapon—something that they could use against the dragon. 'What does this do?' he asked.

Hoodwink frowned at him. 'Duh . . . it's a dagger. You stick it in things,' he said.

'Yes, but what does it *do*?'

The elf prince shrugged. 'Kills stuff.'

'What is its *magical* power?' said Alfie between gritted teeth.

Hoodwink shrugged again. 'Looking nifty, I guess,' he said. 'I suppose you could use it as a reading light.'

While he spoke Derek tied the elf's wrists behind his back. Then she made a ponytail of his hair and held her dagger to it. 'Careful with that,' the elf hissed.

'Or what?' Derek spat. 'Try your spells on me, elf, and you'll be digging my foot out of your nostril.'

'I think that's enough threats, Derek.' Alfie lowered the magical-but-useless dagger with a sigh. 'Come on, let's get back to the Professor and Sir Brenda. But thanks again.'

Derek grunted.

'I thought you hated me?' he continued as they set off.

To Alfie's complete lack of surprise, Derek grunted again.

'I'm only saying because, y'know, saving someone's life is the sort of thing a *friend* would do.'

'Stop talking or I *will* strangle you with your

own tongue,' Derek replied without taking her eyes off the back of Prince Hoodwink's head.

The small procession wound its way through the trees in silence for a while.

'Is that even possible?' Alfie asked, eventually. 'The tongue thing, I mean.'

'You have to stretch it out,' Derek replied. 'A lot.'

'Great. That sort of information is bound to come in handy. Look, Derek, since we're friends now . . .'

'We are *not* friends. This quest is not yet over and you may be useful to me. That is the only reason I saved you.'

'Since we're friends now,' Alfie repeated. 'I *am* going to be useful to you. If we ever make it home I'm going to help you find Skingrath.'

Derek stopped. She turned to stare at Alfie. 'You'll do . . . *what*?' she gasped.

'Yeah,' Alfie nodded, testing the idea in his mind. It felt good. It felt *right*. 'You saved my life. I owe you. There are loads of old books and maps and stuff back at the Unusual Cartography Club headquarters. We'll look for clues and use the club's stone circle to find your god.'

'You'd do that for *me*?' Derek replied. 'Why?'

Alfie shrugged. 'You saved my life. I think that makes you a friend whether you like it or not.'

'But it would be dangerous. You are a non-believer. Skingrath would be upset.'

'I'll risk it.' Alfie insisted.

They trailed on in silence for a while longer. The forest seemed less gloomy now. Dawn was coming, sending a million shafts of sunlight through the leaves. In the distance, Alfie heard the *vip, vip, vip* of arrows, followed by a squawk as some ghastly Hinderwood beast met its end. The elves were already at work, clearing their path.

'Twonk,' Derek said between clenched teeth. 'What I am about to say . . . is difficult. I . . . don't know . . . if . . . I . . . can . . .' Her face scrunched up.

'Come on, Derek. You can do it,' Alfie told her. 'I believe in you.'

Sweating, she hissed, 'I said . . . things . . . earlier. I judged you a weak fool but maybe I was . . . wr-wr-*wrong*. What you . . . what you did tonight:

When you hit this elf. It was not . . . that is to say
. . . it was not *totally* pathetic. You are . . . *different*
. . . but perhaps not completely hopeless. I am
s . . . s. . .'

'Sorry?' Alfie asked.

'Yes, that. *ALL RIGHT*? Are you *happy* now?'

'I am loving this in case anyone's interested,'
Hoodwink chipped in. 'There's going to be kissing
soon, right? Mwah, mwah, mwah. Like that.'

No one *was* interested.

'Happy*ish*. But next time you apologize, try
less snarling,' Alfie said, adding, 'Of course, we'll
have to stop Wrenchpenny tearing down the UCC
headquarters before we go looking for Skingrath,
and I have no idea how to do that. Plus there's still a
dragon to kill.'

Hoodwink stopped. Forgetting the danger to his
hair, he turned. 'You're on a quest to kill the *dragon*?'
he said, blinking. 'Excuse me for a moment, but ha
ha ha ha ha ha HA HA HA HA HA HA HA. You're
so going to die. Oh ho ho, this is *wonderful*. Better
than the hunt. Did I mention HA HA HA HA HA
HA HA?'

'Something funny?' asked Derek, her voice cold.

The elf prince wiped tears of laughter from his eyes. 'Oh yes,' he cackled. 'I should think so. You two, against a dragon. Oh my. What have we got: one under-sixteens body-odour champion and a boy who trips over his own knees. That dragon must be trembling in its scales.'

'Yeah, well, we vanquished *you*,' said Alfie.

Hoodwink's eyes twinkled merrily. 'That might have worked out a bit differently if I was, say, the size of a castle, with heavy armour plating, great big sharp, teeth, and breath that could turn you into a cinder.' Raising his voice he called out, 'Hey Sparklelegs, you'll never guess what.'

'What?' came a voice from the undergrowth.

'They're only off to try and kill the dragon.'

Sparklelegs stood up from where he had been hidden in a bush. He stared at the small group. 'You're pulling my twinkly leg,' he said.

'No, *really*,' Hoodwink chuckled.

'You told them about the huge jaws dripping fire, right? And the armour scales, and the ripping claws.'

'No, I forgot the ripping claws.' Turning back to the questers he said, 'Dragons have ripping claws, too. About twenty of them. Tree-sized. Razor sharp.'

'Sheesh,' said Sparklelegs. 'They should have let *us* kill them. Saved themselves the walk.'

'I seem to remember saying I didn't want to see you,' Alfie growled.

'Oops, sorry.' Sparklelegs ducked back behind his bush, though Alfie could still hear him muttering the word 'weirdoes,' to himself.

Hoodwink lifted his wrists. 'You can untie me now,' he grinned. 'I'm sooo coming to watch. From a safe distance, obviously. It'll be hil-ar-i-*ous*.'

'Shut up,' said Alfie and Derek together.

The elf shut up for a while. In silence, the three of them watched as an elderly woman in a pointed hat shot past them through the air, screeching 'Me wart! Me wart! Flippin' elves cut me wart off,' as she slowly deflated. Hoodwink's folk were doing a good job, Alfie had to admit.

Finally, the elf prince said, 'What's a supermodel?'

CHAPTER TWENTY-TWO
ALFIE'S INCREDIBLE BRAIN

Sir Brenda and the Professor were surprised by the sudden appearance of the elf prince, but enjoyed the easy travel through Hinderwood while elves cleared their path. With no monsters to face and Sparklelegs popping up every so often to point them in the right direction, the journey through the forbidding forest was quite pleasant, except for Hoodwink's endless chatter. 'Sooo' the prince said, two days later. 'On your world these "supermodels" are given lots and lots of gold so ugly people—like you lot—can look at them being beautiful. Is that right?'

'We've been through this a hundred times,' Alfie

groaned as Betsy bounced over yet more roots.

Hoodwink ignored him. 'And they get invited to parties? Loads of parties?'

'Yes.'

'Where the ugly people—like you lot—treat them like gods.'

'Yes.'

'And all they do is look pretty and wear clothes?' said Hoodwink, with a soft whistle. 'That's it?'

'Mmm-hmm,' said Alfie. 'Sometimes just underwear.'

'Your world sounds *brilliant*,' said Hoodwink, thoughtfully.

'It sounds *disgusting*,' Derek interrupted. 'For is it not written that Skingrath will punish the underwear models by peeling their bottoms?'

'I don't know,' said Alfie. '*Is* it written?'

'Probably,' said Derek. 'It's the sort of thing He *would* say.'

'Yes. Yes, it probably is,' said Alfie. 'Now, can we *please* stop talking? I need to *think*. We *still* have to kill a dragon.'

'You'd better think fast,' Hoodwink yawned. 'We're almost there. Look.'

Alfie looked. While they had been talking the trees of Hinderwood had thinned. Up ahead, Sir Brenda brought Thunderhoof to a stop and shielded her eyes against the sunshine. 'Journey's end,' she said quietly, as Betsy pulled up beside her. Hoodwink and Derek stopped next to the old moped. Silently, the questers gazed upon the single lonely mountain that rose before them. It had all the stuff you'd expect to see on a single lonely mountain: forests of pines on the lower slopes, which gave out closer to the top like grandpa's hair; a crooked snowy peak—standard lonely mountain stuff. It also had a dark entrance, about halfway up. From the depths of the mountain poured a plume of black smoke: *dragon* smoke.

Alfie gulped.

Hoodwink giggled. 'And lo the valiant questers did come to Mount Gallyvant where certain death awaited,' he said.

'You're really annoying. You know that, right?' said Alfie.

'Oh yes,' said Hoodwink, nodding. 'That's the whole point.'

Alfie ignored him. 'What do we do now?' he asked aloud. The question that had been bothering him since leaving Verminium still hadn't been answered.

'What choice do we have but to venture forth and attempt to slay the dragon?' sighed Sir Brenda. Face grim, she pulled her sword. Thunderhoof reared up beneath her, the wind catching his mane. Puffing, he dropped back to all-fours, looking pleased with himself. It had been a long time since he'd managed a heroic rear. 'Release the elf,' called Sir Brenda. 'He may return to his home.'

Hoodwink rubbed his wrists as Derek cut the ropes away, then freed his hair and shook it loose. The breeze caught it, setting it streaming about his face and shoulders. It looked fabulous, and the elf prince knew it. 'Ahh, that's better,' he sighed. 'I'm still coming with you, by the way.'

'You'll help us?' asked Alfie.

'Yes,' said Hoodwink. 'By hiding behind a rock. If you *do* manage to kill the dragon I want to try this "modelling".'

'Pitiful,' sniffed Derek.

'On the bright side, if you all die at least you'll be remembered. I'll write a song about you. Elves are good at songs. I'll call it *Some Idiots Went a-Dragonslaying.*'

'Leave it, Derek,' said Alfie as he heard her dagger being drawn. 'He's not worth it.'

Hoodwink snorted, and began singing under his breath.

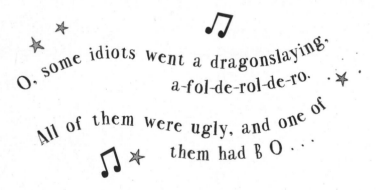

O, some idiots went a dragonslaying,
a-fol-de-rol-de-ro.
All of them were ugly, and one of them had B O . . .

Alfie paid him no attention, staring at the view ahead. Before the questers were two roads. One looked like every other Outlandish road—a winding, muddy track, overgrown with weeds. According to Geeseparty's map it led to the cities and towns of northern Outlandish. The second road made Alfie's bottom hurt just looking at it.

The narrow path was littered with rocks and deep ruts where cartloads of Verminium's gold had been pushed up to the dragon's cave. It was going to do his bruised bum no good at all.

'Onward to glory!' interrupted Sir Brenda, waving her sword.

Thunderhoof clopped onto the path. The Professor twisted Betsy's throttle and the valiant little moped followed with Derek trotting alongside. Behind, Prince Hoodwink skipped along, singing . . .

She really stank, like an old pigsty
And pretty soon she was sure to die.
A fol-de-rol-de . . . ouch!

'My fist slipped,' Derek explained. Alfie sighed and stared up at the entrance to the dragon's cave.

Time was running out.

Despite the Outlandish sunshine he was lost in a dark cloud of defeated misery. Hoodwink was right. They were riding towards their doom. He could see it in Sir Brenda's slumped shoulders. Derek's eyes were fixed on the plume of dragon smoke, while her fingers nervously gripped the hilt of her dagger. For once, the Professor had stopped his usual stream of chatter. He, too, was staring up at the dragon's cave with a worried look on his face. Only Hoodwink was singing happily, while being careful to stay just out of Derek's reach.

Time had run out, and—for once—Alfie's brain had failed to come up with a clever solution.

They were all going to die, except Hoodwink. Hoodwink was going to watch them die then prance away singing a silly song. There was no way they could kill a dragon. There was no way home.

Except.

Except . . .

. . . *Was there?*

Once again, it's time to take a short detour. Every human brain is astounding, you see, and Alfie's was even better than most. For the past thirteen days it hadn't been squatting in his head like a useless grey jelly, taking it easy. No. Deep, deep down, in places Alfie only visited in dreams, his brain had quietly gone into emergency mode. Without Alfie even realizing it, urgent brain meetings had been held, ideas scribbled on the blackboard, and arguments made. Some brain cells had gone off in a huff when their plans were laughed at, but most had stayed at their desks working night and day to get Alfie out of the mess he was in. Their findings had eventually been put to the vote and approved by a majority.

Now, on the very doorstep of danger, the deep, silent part of his brain presented its plan.

Because Alfie's brain cells were quite shy they didn't make a big fuss about it. They just slipped an envelope under the door of Alfie's worried, wakeful, conscious mind.

He opened it.

Instantly, the cloud of misery split open and rolled away. Beams of golden sunshine poured through. Trumpets blared. Angels linked arms and high-kicked across the sky in sandalled feet.

Fireworks exploded, spelling out the words 'Alfie Fleet's Incredible Brain' in blazing letters a hundred metres high. Alfie put his shoulders back and his chin up. He polished his fingernails on his jumper. Once again, his brain had triumphed.

Grinning, he shouted, '*STOP!* I have a *PLAN!*'

Thunderhoof clattered to a halt.

The Professor braked sharply.

Derek skidded to a halt.

Even Hoodwink stopped singing and raised one, perfect, eyebrow.

'A plan for what?' asked the Professor.

'A plan for *everything*,' Alfie said, grinning. 'Professor, you and I are going to get home. The UCC headquarters are going to be fixed up. My mum is going to get her foot spa. Derek, you and I are going to search for Skingrath. Sir Brenda will return home loaded with gold. Hoodwink, you *will* become a famous supermodel.'

'Well done, Rupert,' said the Professor, kick-starting Betsy again. 'That's all sorted then. Off we go.'

'Ah,' interrupted Sir Brenda, holding up a finger.

'One question: how *exactly* are you planning to kill the dragon?

'I'm not,' said Alfie, his grin widening.

'You're thinking of running away, flapping your arms, and screaming, aren't you?' said Sir Brenda. 'I like your style. I really do. But . . .'

'The *Oppressor* told us we had to kill the dragon,' Alfie babbled. 'But he's just a horrible old man who'd give his own daughter away. Why should we do what *he* tells us?'

'Erm . . . is it because the dragon will flame us all to cinders as soon as it sees us?' asked Sir Brenda.

'So what if it *doesn't* see us?' said Alfie. 'Every two weeks it flies off to Verminium to demand more gold. We've been travelling for thirteen days, so that's tomorrow. We can just wait for it to fly off, then grab a load of gold and escape.'

'Eh? Eh? What did he say?' choked the Professor.

'Is he deaf?' asked Hoodwink, who had started plaiting his hair—his own hair, not the Professor's, though, as an interesting side note, if he *had* been plaiting the Professor's hair it would have meant they were married under Elvish law. Without waiting for a reply, Hoodwink raised his voice, and shouted, 'The ugly boy said *you don't have to kill the dragon. YOU DON'T HAVE TO KILL THE DRAGON.* Hey, has anyone ever told you that you look just like a Pathetic Wanja Bird?'

'I'm worshipped as a god on fourteen planets, you know,' the Professor grumbled.

'But if we *don't* kill the dragon, the Oppressor will have me thrown in the dungeon,' interrupted Sir Brenda.

'Oh dear,' said Alfie. 'Getting thrown in a dungeon. That's a *lot* worse than getting burned to a crisp and crunched up by a dragon, isn't it?'

'Actually, I know sixteen ways to escape the Verminium Palace dungeons,' muttered Sir Brenda. 'Probably should've remembered that. Or I could just overthrow the Oppressor. It wouldn't be difficult. No one likes him very much. But . . . but . . . the dragon will still burn Verminium.'

'You're Outlandish's greatest hero,' said Alfie. 'I'm sure you'll work it out.'

Sir Brenda looked thoughtful. 'A new quest,' she said eventually. 'I like the sound of that. It would be a *great* quest, too. I could round up another band of adventurers. *Proper* adventurers this time. Herkleton could even charge them a joining fee. There would be hooded cloaks and everything. Probably even magic rings. And if . . . *when* . . . we were successful, the people of Verminium would make me queen. That might be nice. We could move into the palace. I know Herkleton misses indoor toilets.'

'But I am ready to fight,' Derek chipped in. 'I have spent many nights praying to Skingrath for the strength to kill this dragon.'

'Stop whining Derek,' Alfie said. Looking around, he continued, 'So, are we all in agreement? We wait for the dragon to fly off then grab some gold and make a run for it?'

Three heads nodded. Derek shrugged and looked sulky.

And so, Alfie Fleet's incredible brain had saved the day. Or had it? If you remember, Alfie had a date with the dragon that had been fated the second he clapped eyes upon the great beast. Perhaps the journey back to London wasn't going to be quite as easy as he thought . . .

CHAPTER TWENTY-THREE
FAREWELL TO OUTLANDISH

At the foot of Mount Gallyvant the questers found
a small hollow, ringed by pine trees where they
could rest for the night. Camped out on the dragon's
doorstep, they finished the jar of pickled eggs Sir
Brenda had brought along while the Outlandish
moons rose in the sky, riding on wisps of drifting
dragon smoke. Soon, Sir Brenda, Derek, and
Hoodwink were snoring beneath blankets while
Alfie and the Professor gazed into the campfire,
silently.

In just a few hours Alfie was going into a
dragon's cave where the lost stone circle would
take him to Brains-in-Jars World. From there the

path to home—and his mum—lay open. Sleep was impossible. He was *way* too excited. Instead, he opened his notebook. By the golden light of the flickering fire, Alfie turned the pages, looking back at the notes and sketches he'd made during the journey across Outlandish. He'd always dreamed of adventuring across a strange and magical world, like the people in his favourite books. His dreams had come true. Alright, so Hoodwink wasn't what he'd been expecting, but watching a dragon fly had been amazing. Plus he'd seen actual magic, nearly gotten into a fight with villainous rogues in a tumbledown inn, visited old castles, and met a wizard. All in all, it had been an incredible trip.

And now it was nearly over. Alfie felt an unexpected pang of sadness. He desperately wanted to get home to his mum, but getting home meant his adventure would be at an end.

With a sigh, Alfie turned another page of his notebook . . .

THE UNUSUAL TRAVEL AGENCY?

The words he'd scribbled down outside the Oppressor's palace in Verminium stared at him. Alfie had forgotten all about them.

He blinked.

The Unusual Travel Agency . . .

As if his marvellous brain hadn't already done enough that day, it suddenly sparkled with a new idea. Maybe getting home needn't be the end of his adventure. Maybe it could be the *start* of a hundred more. Alfie reached into Betsy's saddlebag and pulled out *The Cosmic Atlas*. It contained maps and charts for more than three hundred worlds. Alfie turned pages past a map of Blysss, a world of tropical, sandy islands; the snowy mountains of Brrrrchillyoutagain where the ski season would last forever; Nerwong Nerwong Plinky-Plonk with its temples dotted throughout endless jungle; Win'span—a world with little gravity where people glided from place to place on homemade wings . . .

Every page offered fresh possibilities for fun and adventure.

Alfie wanted to visit them all. And if *he* wanted to see them, so would other people. *Lots* of other people. The stone circle beneath Wigless Square could send humans from Earth to all of these planets, and if there wasn't one they liked in *The Cosmic Atlas* then the Professor could open up an Explorer's Pathway and *discover* the perfect place for them. The infinite universe held endless surprises, after all. The three hundred worlds in *The Cosmic Atlas* were just a start.

After a while, Alfie took a pencil from his pocket. He sucked the end for a few moments, then started writing.

Hearing the rustle of paper and Alfie's scribbling pencil, the Professor turned his head.

'Ah, Rupert,' the old man said. 'Can't sleep either, eh? Can't wait to get home to your mum, I expect.'

'Something like that,' said Alfie, lifting his head. 'How about you?'

'I was wondering what will become of the Unusual Cartography Club,' sighed the Professor. 'I mean, it's just me now, producing a book that no one will ever read. What's the point of it all? I was getting a bit miserable, to be honest. Silly really. But

I'm an old man now and old men are often silly. You'll probably find you're quite silly, too, once you get to my age. You start out, as a young person, not silly at all, and then . . . *bang* . . . you wake up one day to find that you've become silly. I think it's something to do with . . .'

'I don't think you're silly,' Alfie interrupted. 'As it happens, I was thinking about the UCC, too. It *would* be sad if you were the last ever President.'

'Maybe I *should* just go into an old peoples' home,' the Professor continued with a sigh. 'Grow some cucumbers.'

'You could do that, I suppose,' said Alfie, tapping the page of his notebook where he'd been writing. 'Or using my bold plan you could open an exciting new chapter in the UCC's history.'

'What? What are you talking about, Rupert?' The Professor asked. 'Oh wait . . . you're going to bring up all that travel guide nonsense again, aren't you?'

'Would a guide book be so bad?' Alfie replied. There's only so much gold we'll be able to carry, and fixing up the UCC headquarters will be expensive. You know that, don't you? Oh, you'll probably be able to grab enough to keep the place going for a while. But sooner or later the money will run out again and the UCC will be forced to close.'

'Yes, but like I said there's no one to keep it open *for*,' said the Professor with a sad shrug. 'Just a silly old man with his maps and moped. What's the point of a club with no members?'

'There's me,' said Alfie. 'If you'll have me, I'd join the Unusual Cartography Club in a heartbeat.'

'You would?' The Professor blinked, surprised. 'But I thought you'd had a *ghastly* time. People trying to kill us every five minutes, *and* I forgot to pack the toilet roll. *Ghastly*. You must have *hated* it.'

'Are you kidding? It's been *brilliant*,' said Alfie, his eyes glowing in the torchlight. 'I mean, I've *really* missed my mum, so next time we could try not getting stranded and maybe cut down on the certain-death side of things, but it's been *amazing*. *You're* amazing. I'd *love* to explore more worlds with you. Derek too, I should think. I've got a feeling she's never going back to her people.'

'You'd like to join the UCC, Rupert? *Really?*' Tears brimmed in the Professor's eyes. 'I could pass the ancient knowledge down to the next generation. Show you some *incredible* places. That would make an old man very happy. Very happy indeed.'

'But the UCC would have to make money or it would all collapse again, sooner or later,' said Alfie. 'We needn't stop at a guide book, either. I had an idea back in Verminium. You once told me that people used circles to go on holiday, back in the old days. Why can't we use the circle in Wigless Square the same way? People pay a lot for exotic trips so why not reopen the Unusual Cartography Club as the Unusual *Travel Agency*? We could send tourists to amazing worlds, and charge them money: *loads* of money. Plus, there would be a gift shop and book sales. Well, look.' He held out the notebook, adding, 'I've worked out how much we could make. This would be just the beginning. It could be a *lot* more, especially once the Unusual Travel Agency got bigger.'

U *T* *A*

THE UNUSUAL TRAVEL AGENCY

A UNIVERSE OF SURPRISES AWAITS . . .

50 tourists per day at £500 each

+ gift shop (t-shirts, mugs, souvenirs, elf hair-care products, etc)

+ sales of *The Cosmic Atlas* and guide books

+ guided tours

= roughly £30,000 per day

= about £10,950,000 per year

The Professor gasped. 'Ten million nine hundred and fifty thousand *pounds*?' he squawked. 'Per *year*?'

'That would just be the start. There's so much we could do. With the time differences we could offer weekend breaks that last a fortnight,' said Alfie, excitedly. 'Or even holidays people could take in their lunch hour. And Sir Brenda could expand her business, too. Loads of people play quests in video games. She'd make a fortune offering *real* adventures, and we could take a fee. I've been looking through *The Cosmic Atlas* and there are hundreds of interesting planets we could send people to. And we could build more circles, all over the world—all over the *universe*. Humans could start exploring again. They'd probably put up another statue of you. Get the nose right this time . . .'

'Hmm, a seventy-foot Bowell-Mouvemont in the middle of the city,' said the Professor. 'That *would* be something special, but this is all a bit much, Rupert. We're *supposed* to be a serious research institute, you know? Not some awful *business*. What would Samantha Sibilant say? Or Madelaine Tusk? Or Jimmy Whuppley, or old Davy Gitspew?'

'They're gone,' said Alfie, gently. 'And soon the UCC will be, too. It really is too amazing to be lost forever, but you can save it and there could still be a research department. There would always be new worlds to discover, and *The Cosmic Atlas* would still need updating. We could give it a new design, too. Make it relevant for a modern, younger audience.

You could be in charge of that.'

'I . . . I know you want to help, Rupert,' the Professor stammered. 'And you've certainly proved yourself to be intelligent. You've helped us out of some terrible scrapes, eh? But I'm an *explorer*, what do I know about *business*?' groaned the Professor. 'It's all hair gel and fashionable spectacles and being a greedy, thieving toad, isn't it?'

'Not all businesses are like that,' said Alfie. 'I've read a lot about them. And you could afford to hire people for the day-to-day stuff. My mum could run the gift shop. She *hates* working at the fish factory. You'd be doing us a huge favour. We really are very poor, you know, and the Unusual Travel Agency could easily afford to give mum a pay rise.'

'It would be my pleasure to give you and your mum any help I could Rupert, but . . . but . . . centuries of UCC tradition would be swept away. It would be . . . *awful*, Rupert. Awful.'

'You *are* the president, Professor, so it's your decision. If you prefer cucumbers, and being lifted on and off the toilet at Wrenchpenny's old people's home . . .'

'When you put it like that, maybe I *should* think about it,' said the Professor.

'There's no need to make a decision right now,' Alfie replied. 'But it's going to be a long night. Could we get started on passing down all that ancient knowledge?'

CHAPTER TWENTY-FOUR
A SEA OF BLING

The dragon emerged from its lair, morning sunlight glittering on crimson scales as it sniffed the air. Smoke curled from its nostrils. Crouched behind a rock, Alfie held his breath as he watched. The creature was even more magnificent—and more frightening—than he remembered. Trumpeting a stone-shattering roar, it launched itself into the sky. The *thud, thud, thud* of vast wings echoed across the landscape as it flew away over the green line on the horizon that was Hinderwood.

Alfie gulped. This was it. The dragon was gone. All that stood between him and home was a staircase that led into its lair and a ride across Brains-in-Jars World.

His heart beating at the speed of a road drill, he went to fetch his companions.

It took half an hour to heave Betsy up the staircase but eventually the questers stood at the entrance to the dragon's lair. Immediately, Derek fell to her knees, staring up at the giant entrance into the dragon's cave. Alfie followed her gaze. Among the carved creatures that decorated the arch was a three-headed creature with hair of fire. 'Skingrath,' she whispered. 'You were not lying, Wanja-faced old man. This truly *is* the path to His realm.'

'Yes, and it's the path to many other realms, too,' the Professor chuckled, pointing. 'The six-legged maggot thing with all the teeth up there is a Pulsating Swib. Wonderful, gentle, creatures. They love having their soft undergiblets tickled. Over there, with the crown that looks like a toad—that's the Spang-flavoured Emperor of Triple-Falange . . .'

'*Professor*, the dragon could come back at any time,' Alfie interrupted.

'Of course, of course, of course. No time to waste, eh? Come along then.'

Trembling, Alfie pushed Betsy onwards, into

an echoing tunnel, carved with the landscapes of bizarre worlds. Light from Sir Brenda's flaming torch sparkled off crystals clustered like galaxies in the ceiling above. Hoodwink looked around. 'What is this place?' he asked. 'It's quite impressive, I suppose. If you like that sort of thing.'

'It must have been an important circle in its day,' whispered the Professor. 'It's not often you see this kind of decoration. Probably had thousands of people coming and going, travelling to every corner of the universe on their holidays. Sticky children wearing hats and clutching their parents' hands. Excited chatter. Informative guide books containing serious information. New worlds opening up every day . . .'

Alfie smiled to himself. It sounded like the Professor had been doing some thinking.

'If you think that's a sight, wait until you catch an eyeful of this,' Sir Brenda gasped.

Alfie almost dropped the old moped as he stopped beside the knight. Derek took a deep breath. Even Hoodwink blinked. 'Woo, that's a *lot* of gold,' the elf whispered.

The great circular cavern where the dragon had made its home was straight out of the wildest fairy tale. If he hadn't seen it with his own eyes, Alfie wouldn't have believed the universe contained such riches. The crystal stars that decorated the ceiling sparkled down on a sea of treasure. Glittering waves spread to every wall: coins and great bars of gold, jewellery, golden statues of forgotten gods, the crowns of long-dead kings and queens, fist-sized diamonds, and rubies, and sapphires . . . enough treasure to buy entire worlds, and still have enough change for lunch at a really good restaurant.

Alfie took it all in with one dazed glance, then fixed his eyes on the giant stone circle at the centre of the cavernous chamber. It was at least three times the size of the circle beneath Wigless Square, and perfect in every way. Rising from the golden ocean, its pillars supported a complete ring of cap stones. At the centre stood a stone table. Tears in his eyes, Alfie tore his gaze away and looked up at the Professor. 'We did it,' he croaked. 'We found it.'

The Professor laid a hand on his shoulder. 'Yes, Rupert, we found it,' he said. 'It's a beauty, too.'

Alfie stooped and picked up a single golden coin. 'And we're rich,' he said.

Ching.

Moving the coin set off a small avalanche of coins. *Ching, ching, ching,* they went: *ching-ching-chingetty-ching.*

A golden tide swept around Alfie's ankles. 'Hey, Derek—' he began.

His voice was cut off by a roar. A roar that came from five hundred miles away. A roar of planet-breaking fury. The mountain trembled, setting off more avalanches of gold.

The coin fell from Alfie's fingers. 'Oh,' he said, as the roar died away. 'What's happening now?'

'I'm no expert,' said Hoodwink, 'but my guess is that dragons have quite good hearing and *really* don't like people touching their treasure.'

'Oh,' said Alfie again. 'That's bad.'

'How fast can dragons fly, I wonder?' asked Sir Brenda, fingering the hilt of her sword.

'Fast, I'll bet,' said Hoodwink.

'Not a problem,' said the Professor, striding forward. 'Sir Brenda, I took some new coordinates just outside Verminium. If you'll follow us I can use the circle at home to open an Explorer's Pathway and drop you just outside the city gates.' He turned to Hoodwink. 'Prince . . . Prince . . . oh, what's your name? No, don't tell me. Prince *Munchwinkle*—I knew I'd get it. Prince Munchwinkle, if you'd care to step this way, too. All aboard for Brains-in-Jars World. Toot toot.'

The elf scowled. '*What* did he call me?'

'Doesn't matter, let's get out of here,' Alfie yelped, pushing Betsy towards the circle. 'Everyone grab some gold and *move*.'

The roar came again, closer this time. Dust showered down from the ceiling. Panting, Alfie shoved the moped forward, wading through treasure. Tinkling gold weighed down his every step while the dragon's screams grew louder, and louder still. Alfie could hear a thrumming noise beneath them now: vast wings beating with hummingbird speed, powering the furious dragon back to its golden nest.

However fast a dragon could fly though, it wasn't fast enough. Laughing with relief, Alfie reached the stone circle first. Glancing back to make sure his companions were close behind he stuffed handfuls of gold and jewels into his pockets, then shoved an enormous diamond down the front of his trousers. Finally, with a grin, he gripped Betsy's handlebars, and pushed her between the stones.

Once again the dragon's furious roar shook Mount Gallyvant. Alfie shut his eyes and waited for the universe to unfold around him, taking him far, far away from the deadly beast.

Nothing happened.

Well, not *completely* nothing. A new sound echoed in Alfie's ears: the sound of the Professor saying 'Oh poot.'

CHAPTER TWENTY-FIVE
HOW NOT TO KILL
A DRAGON

Alfie's laugh died. He waited, eyes squeezed shut, heart beating a drum solo. There couldn't be something wrong with the circle after all they had been through. There just *couldn't*. It was old. Maybe it just needed a little longer . . .

'Tsk,' tutted the Professor. 'Well, *really*. I mean to say. If that doesn't just top it all.'

Alfie opened his eyes to see the Professor fiddling with the underside of the stone table at the centre of the circle. 'Problem?' he asked in a squeaky voice.

'It's not activated,' the Professor huffed. 'Whoever used it last left it on standby. The dratted thing must have switched itself off after a century or two.'

Alfie's reply was lost in the depths of a mountain-cracking dragon roar.

As it echoed away, Thunderhoof neighed. Vaulting onto his back, Sir Brenda flipped her visor down and drew her sword. 'So, it seems we must do battle after all,' she said in a muffled voice. 'It is an honour to stand beside you all in our hour of doom, noble companions.'

'Whatever,' said Prince Hoodwink, looking around. 'Hiding time, I think.'

'Pathetic,' Derek growled.

'Can you fix it?' Alfie shouted to the Professor.

'Oh yes, I haven't spent a lifetime in the Unusual Cartography Club without picking up a few tricks,' said the Professor, dusting off his hands on his trousers. 'It'll just take a few moments to jump start, but these older models need half an hour to warm up.' He sucked his moustache before adding, 'Give or take a minute or two.'

'I don't think we have a minute or two,' Alfie squeaked. The sound of scrabbling claws echoed down the main tunnel. The dragon had landed. 'Do dragons have any weak spots, Sir Brenda?' he asked in a wobbling voice.

Sir Brenda shrugged with a clank of armour. 'Who knows? No one's ever killed one before.'

'There's a first time for everything,' Derek grunted. Pulling her dagger from its sheath, she fell into a fighting crouch.

'I'm off. You all have fun with the screaming and dying,' Hoodwink chipped in, snatching up a crown and holding it up. 'Do you think this will suit me, by the way? I think the emeralds will really make my eyes pop.'

Sir Brenda's visor turned toward him. 'The boy was right: you are *very* annoying,' she said.

'Impishly charming, I *think* you'll find,' sniffed the elf. With a wink, he turned and fled down a small, dark tunnel behind the circle.

Alfie gazed after him. There was another tunnel. Dimly he remembered seeing it on Geeseparty's map. The tunnel was a dead end, but it was somewhere they could hide. 'No fighting,' Alfie yelled. Dropping Betsy, he stumbled after the elf.

'We'll be safe down there. It's too small for the dragon.'

Unfortunately, his voice was again drowned out by another rage-filled roar. As you may remember, Alfie was destined to meet the dragon, and destiny can *never* be avoided. Before he had time to shout again, the dragon's head filled the chamber's entrance: a head crowned with vicious spikes. Teeth like sharpened gravestones filled its gaping mouth. Coiling flame leapt from its nostrils. Slit eyes, burning from white hot to boiling orange—glared at the questers as the head snaked this way and that at the end of a long, scaled neck.

THIEVES!

'*THIEVES!*' the dragon roared in a voice that toppled statues.

Alfie's jaw dropped open. Burning eyes fixed on him from high above. A small part of his brain told him it was glad he had taken the time to empty his bladder before setting out.

'Um . . . we're not thieves,' he squeaked, backing towards the tunnel. 'We just w-wanted to use the stone circle. We weren't going to s-steal anything.' At that moment the pockets of Alfie's charity shop jeans burst, showering gold coins on the floor. 'I have literally *no* idea how they got in there,' he finished, blushing.

'*THIEVES!*' the dragon repeated. Rearing, it opened its mouth. Fire bubbled at the back of its throat.

'Gah,' Alfie murmured, shrinking back. As last words go, it wasn't very inspiring.

Luckily, it wasn't to be his last word. As flames filled the dragon's mouth Derek shouted, 'Hey, dragon twonk.'

The dragon's head swept round, spewing flame. Alfie gawped as Derek ducked beneath the torrent of fire. Then, she jumped. Snatching at the crest lining the beast's head she vaulted astride its neck and stabbed down with a double-handed blow that *should* have speared the dragon's brain.

Her blade shattered on its scales instead.

With a toss of its head, the dragon shook her off.

Derek hit the wall and rolled out of the way as jaws snapped closed where she had landed half a second before. The dragon's tail lashed from the other direction. It smashed into her, sending her spinning back into the wall with bone-crunching force.

'*Derek!*' Alfie shrieked, wading towards her crumpled body through chinking gold.

'Amateurs,' Sir Brenda muttered. 'Let's show 'em how it's done, my steed.' Her heels touched Thunderhoof's sides. The old horse leapt into battle: mane flowing, eyes blazing, and hooves lashing.

'Get the girl into the tunnel,' Sir Brenda yelled, ducking a swipe of the dragon's claws. With a *whhhuuuuum* sound, her sword swept through the air and clashed against the dragon's snout. 'Hurrah for Sir Brenda!' she bellowed, holding it aloft. 'The greatest adventurer on Outlandish. Dragon, prepare to meet your doo—'

A perfectly aimed blast of flame melted her sword. Yelping, she dropped the glowing remains and shook her hand, squealing, 'Ow, ow, ow, owwwww.'

'What were you saying, *thief*?' sneered the dragon.

Alfie reached Derek and pulled her to her feet. She staggered upright, clutching her ribs. Tossing aside the useless hilt of her dagger, she cracked her knuckles. '*Right*,' she said, lunging at the dragon. 'I'm going to break your *face*.'

Alfie threw himself at her legs. The two of them went down in a shower of gold. 'Get off me,' Derek growled.

'Not. Going. To. *Happen*,' Alfie panted, getting a face full of stinking furs as he wrestled her down. Grabbing an ankle, he strained to pull her towards the tunnel entrance.

Derek kicked him off, scrabbling to her knees on shifting piles of gold. 'I don't need *saving*,' she panted.

'You'll *die*.'

'I am prepared to meet Skingrath.'

'When you meet Skingrath, I'm gonna be right beside you,' Alfie grunted as she elbowed him in the stomach.

'Probably,' Derek admitted. 'In about ten seconds or less.'

Between them and the dragon, Sir Brenda wheeled

Thunderhoof, dodging blasts of fire and deadly
claws. Without a weapon the fight was no fight at
all. Above her, the dragon reared back for the killer
blow. Thudding wings sent an expensive tornado of
golden coins whirling around the chamber. Alfie and
Derek covered their faces.

The dragon lashed out with claws that raked a shower of sparks across Sir Brenda's armour. Ripped steel crunching on gold, she was thrown from Thunderhoof's saddle and rolled, groaning, to Alfie's feet.

The dragon reared again, its mouth a cave of fire.

'Sorry mum,' Alfie murmured to himself, looking up into the gaping jaws of flaming death. He felt something brush against his fingers. Glancing down, he saw with some surprise that it was Derek's hand.

The Skingrathian girl twisted her fingers tightly in his as she gazed up into the dragon's fiery jaws. 'Friend,' she whispered.

'Yeah,' said Alfie, giving her hand a squeeze. He smiled. 'But—y'know—more like a sister, really.'

As last words go, those were much better.

Alfie looked up as death came hurtling towards him.

And then, with a shriek of rage the dragon fell back, claws batting a sudden hail of arrows that were *vip-vip-vipping* towards its eyes.

'Who's pathetic now, smelly?' Prince Hoodwink crowed from the tunnel entrance as he loosed arrow after arrow with deadly accuracy until his fingers found the quiver on his back empty. 'Quick, ugly people. Into the tunnel.'

Derek's fingers jerked from Alfie's. Hurling herself at the dragon with fists curled and teeth bared, she tripped over Sir Brenda's suddenly outstretched out leg.

Alfie looked at Sir Brenda as Derek sprawled between them.

Sir Brenda looked at Alfie and staggered to her feet.

They both nodded.

Taking an ankle each, they dragged Derek—struggling and spitting—into the tunnel. With a backwards glance, Alfie saw the dragon's massive head rushing towards them again, flame flooding over its gaping jaws. Then everything was scorching heat and the smell of singed hair. Somehow, his legs kept moving as fire flooded down the tunnel. Screaming, he flapped his spare arm to put the fire on his jumper out.

'Good lad,' shouted Sir Brenda. 'Running away, screaming, and flapping your arms. Nice moves.'

Derek's ankle gripped tightly in his hand, Alfie followed Hoodwink into the cool depths of the dark tunnel. As he ran, a thought crossed his mind . . .

Where was the Professor?

CHAPTER TWENTY-SIX

DRAGON'S DEN

Alfie's question was immediately answered. 'I've met some horrible creatures in my time,' the Professor's voice said, echoing down the dark passage. 'Giant, man-eating lobsters, the Irritating Weevil Folk of Infestia Six, Wrenchpenny from the council, and so on—but *you*, dragon, are the worst of them . . .'

'What's he doing?' asked Prince Hoodwink.

'Sounds like he's giving the dragon a telling-off,' answered Sir Brenda. 'A nasty one, too. Good for him.'

'How *dare* you take over an important historic site for your own personal use?' the Professor's voice continued. 'And how *dare* you attack my companions? I warn you that you do *not* want to annoy me. No one wants an angry Bowell-Mouvemont on their hands and I am *extremely* close to losing my temper.'

'He's trying to buy us time,' said Alfie. 'The circle needs half an hour to warm up. If we can just keep the dragon busy . . .'

'You are a thin, scrawny-looking thief,' the dragon's voice purred, interrupting Alfie. 'But tasty, I should think. Shall we find out?'

'Eating a Bowell-Mouvemont is not recommended,' replied the Professor. 'You'll find us unexpectedly chewy . . .'

In the darkness of the tunnel Derek propped herself up against the wall, clutching her ribs. 'The old man is braver than I thought,' she said. 'But he will fail.'

'We have to help him,' said Alfie, desperately. '*I* have to help him.'

A burning eye filled the end of the tunnel with heart-stopping suddenness. Alfie stared into a black slit of inky wickedness edged with boiling fire. The dragon chuckled. 'Your companion is trapped,' it rumbled. 'And you are trapped, too. There is no other way out of this tunnel. So I offer you this deal. Starve while listening to his screams as I eat him piece by piece, or come out of your hole and I will kill you all quickly.'

'The Wanja-faced old man did not lie to me,' Derek wheezed. 'For that he deserves a quick death. I shall go.'

'I, too,' said Sir Brenda. 'It may be that I can still defeat this foul worm.'

In the gloom, Hoodwink sighed. 'You've got no weapons, you prannet. What are you going to do— knee it in the goolies?'

'If it has goolies, I have knees,' Sir Brenda said.

'We shall *all* go, at least we will die fighting,' said Derek.

'Better idea,' said Hoodwink. 'You lot die fighting, I'll sneak out while you keep it busy.'

'No,' Alfie said, firmly. 'No one is going to die. You lot stay here.'

'Alfie . . . *no*,' Derek croaked as he walked down the tunnel, silhouetted against the dragon's glaring eye.

It was too late. The dragon's eye withdrew. Alfie walked out into its lair.

Derek struggled to her feet to go after him, only to be pulled back by Sir Brenda. 'Trust the boy,' the knight said, softly. 'I have seen this sort of thing before. He has been touched by destiny. Happens all the time on quests.'

'But I've seen him fight,' hissed Derek. 'He's *useless*. He'll *die*.'

'Watch,' whispered Sir Brenda. 'Destiny is at work.'

Alfie's bizarre knees almost gave out as he looked up into burning eyes high above him. They flickered with *greed*. It gave Alfie an idea. He needed to keep the dragon talking and he had seen the same look in the eyes of many people on the covers of magazines like *Isn't Money Brilliant*? He glanced at the Professor. The old man stood before the giant stone circle with his hands on his hips and his moustache bristling with outrage, unhurt. Alfie flicked his eyes from the Professor's to the circle, and back again, in an unspoken question: *is it on*?

The Professor gave him a small nod, opening and

closing his hand five times. Twenty-five minutes until the circle was working. 'Now look here, Rupert,' the old man said. 'I don't like giving orders but as your expedition leader, I *order* you to return to safety in that tunnel. Very quickly. Very quickly *indeed* . . .'

'It's all right Professor, I've got this,' said Alfie. He looked up at the dragon. 'Hi,' he said.

'Hello,' said the dragon. 'And goodbye.' It opened its mouth and took a breath, gathering flame at the back of its throat.

'As you seem to like deals,' said Alfie, 'I have one for you.'

The dragon paused. '*You* have a deal for *me*?' it rasped. 'But your death is all I want, *thief*, and I have that already.'

'Your loss,' said Alfie with a shrug. 'Because it's not all you want, is it? What you *really* want is more gold. *Much* more gold. And I can get it for you.'

CHAPTER TWENTY-SEVEN

EXIT NEGOTIATIONS

The dragon blinked.

'Interested?' Alfie said, trying to keep the squeak out of his voice.

'You are not a small patch of soot on the floor,' said the dragon. 'Does that answer your question, *thief*?'

Alfie nudged a pile of gold coins with his foot. 'This is all very pretty,' he said. 'Glittery and tinkly and all that, but it's very old-fashioned, don't you think?'

'A cavern full of gold never really goes out of style,' rumbled the dragon. 'What is your point?'

Alfie bent and picked up a single gold coin. The

dragon hissed.

Alfie held the gold piece up. It twinkled. 'There are better things to do with so much money than leave it lying around,' he said. 'But if gold is what you like then I could turn this into a hundred like it,' he said. 'I could turn a hundred into a thousand, a thousand into ten thousand, and so on. I could set more gold flowing into this chamber than you have ever dreamed of and you wouldn't have to lift a finger . . . er . . . vicious-looking claw.'

The dragon's eyes narrowed. 'You are a thief *and* a liar,' it sneered.

Alfie let the coin drop from his fingers. Shaking his head, he stared up at the dragon. 'I'm not lying,' he said. 'Tell me, do you understand the words "liquidity" and "leverage"? How about "*investment*"?'

The dragon hissed again. 'What demonic spell is this?'

'Not a spell. *Business*. Let me explain.' Taking his time, Alfie pulled the gramophone from around his neck. He set it on the floor in front of him, then placed his crash helmet next to it. Finally, he took a seat on a mound of gold and pulled his notebook and pencil from his pocket. 'Let's start with stocks and shares . . .'

Flipping open the notebook Alfie began to talk, in a patient, unhurried voice. Minutes ticked by as he explained the idea of buying a share in a business then taking some of the money the business made. More minutes fluttered past while he told the dragon about his plans for the Unusual Cartography Club. Even more as he scribbled in his notebook, working out how much gold the Unusual Travel Agency profits would buy. Finally, he held up the pad and showed it to the dragon.

The dragon's eyes widened. 'A remarkable amount of gold,' it purred. 'And you would give me a *share*?'

Alfie nodded. 'You'd have to make an investment first, of course,' he said, making more calculations. 'Five hundred pieces of gold should be enough. But the profits would increase over time, so you'd get back much more than that. *Much* more. You'd be richer than ever. There would be no need to burn cities or eat anyone ever again.' Alfie stopped and looked up at the dragon. 'What do you think?'

'Congratulations, thief,' purred the dragon after a moment or two of silence. 'You have my interest.'

'Great,' said Alfie, flipping to a fresh page in his notebook. 'I'll start drawing up a contract, shall I? A fifteen percent share in the Unusual Travel Agency in return for your investment . . .'

'*Fifteen* percent?'

'I might have a little wriggle room on that,' Alfie said. 'Let's call it seventeen and a half. We'll have to add some stuff to the contract, of course. You'll agree to let my friends go free. That's a standard clause and goes without saying. Plus, with your new stream of income you'll no longer need to set fire to Verminium every couple of weeks, so we we'll add a "no terrorizing" paragraph—'

The very tip of a razor-sharp claw knocked the book from Alfie's hand. '*Or*,' the dragon interrupted. 'We could say I make no "investment" at all, but you bring me *one hundred* percent of your profits. In the meantime, your companions will stay here. If in one *week's* time I am unhappy with the amount of gold you bring me then I will eat one, another the following week, and so on. Oh, and I will also *continue* to terrorize Verminium. That's a standard clause. Goes without saying.'

'OK, look, I don't think you've really got the hang of this but I can go up to twenty five percent,' Alfie said. 'But only if we can nail down the friends-go-free thing.'

'You've heard my final offer,' said the dragon. 'Take it or leave it.'

'Forty percent. Fifty . . . Honestly, you'll make *more* money investing,' Alfie said. 'Stop killing people. Join the modern world.'

Wisps of smoke rose from the dragon's nostrils. 'I *like* killing people,' it said. 'It's fun. So, accept my offer or die.'

'Let me think about it for a moment,' said Alfie, desperately, glancing at the Professor.

The old man flashed Alfie two fingers, shaking his head.

'You have ten seconds,' the dragon yawned. 'Nine, eight, seven . . .'

Alfie picked up the Unusual Cartography Club's translating device, and began turning the handle. 'You're sure that's your choice?' he asked, desperately. 'It doesn't need to be like this . . .'

'Four, three, two . . .'

'OK, I've made my decision,' said Alfie.

'Wise,' purred the dragon. 'So, you will return to me in one week loaded with gold and . . .'

The handle of the translator snapped off in Alfie's hand. Instantly, the little device grew warmer, heating up with every passing second. It started making a faint whining noise. 'My decision is no,' he said, quietly. 'No deal.'

The dragon reared back in surprise. 'Are you *mad*,' it hissed.

The broken translator started shrieking. 'No,' Alfie said. 'But I *do* have the upper hand in this negotiation. Sorry about what happens next. Really sorry. I wish I didn't have to do it.'

'You *will* be sorry, but not for very long.' The dragon's head dived towards Alfie. Eyes dancing with flames of vicious glee, it opened its mouth like a striking snake, ready to pour a deadly cascade of fire.

Alfie pulled his arm back.

And just before the dragon could release its blast

of flame he hurled the Unusual Cartography Club's translating gizmo, doodah, thingy, down its throat.

CHAPTER TWENTY-EIGHT
THE BEAST EXPLODES

An exploding dragon is never a pretty sight, but—
in this case at least—it doesn't happen all at once.
Madelaine Tusk's Universal Translator melted on
contact with the dragon's fiery venom, producing
an explosion—just as the Professor had told Alfie
would happen if the device was broken. The
dragon's heavy scales contained the first blast,
though the explosion had to be released from
somewhere. It farted: a dynamite fart that sounded
like the dragon had stepped on an enormous duck;
a fiery, jet-engine bum parp that sent the huge beast
screaming across the chamber where it hit the wall
in a tangle of wings and tail. To repeat: it wasn't a
pretty sight.

The dragon sat up shaking its dazed head while chunks of the ceiling dropped on it from above. Then it burped a ball of fire.

Alfie threw himself into a heap of gold as the fireball ripped past overhead, and came up shouting:

'The circle.

RUUUUUN!'

The first blast now set off a chain reaction with the dragon's fiery venom. It entered the second stage of explosion, the dragon slithering to its feet as a dull detonation went off deep within its stomach, followed by another, then another, as if it had eaten a bad prawn. The dragon's body swelled to twice its normal size.

33

Fiery cracks appeared between its scales. Then it shrank, then swelled again as it clamped its mouth shut, trying to contain the blasts within. It farted again: this time a squeaky, peeping high-pitched fart that told Alfie its mouth wasn't the only thing the dragon was trying to keep clamped shut.

Snatching up his motorbike helmet, Alfie staggered across shifting piles of gold, eyes fixed on the Professor, who was hopping from one foot to the other, yelping 'I say, I say, I say.' As he passed the moped, Alfie grabbed Betsy's handlebars. Pulling her upright, he heaved the old machine towards the gigantic stone circle. Risking a glance over his shoulder, he saw that the dragon was experiencing the third and final stage of its explosion. Now, it now looked like a scaly balloon with stubby wings. It was spinning on the spot, eyes wide with surprise, and its tail stiff with fear. The glowing cracks between its scales had widened, straining apart as the explosions in its stomach built, and built.

Thunderhoof burst from the tunnel entrance, hooves kicking up a storm of gold. Sir Brenda hunched over the horse's neck, galloping at the circle as Derek clung on behind. Beside them leapt Hoodwink, cloak billowing and his hair streaming beneath his new crown. He looked pretty darned snazzy and judging by the grin on his face he knew it too.

With the Professor pointing the way, the horse leapt through two standing stones. In an eye-blink, Thunderhoof disappeared.

A cheer escaped Alfie's mouth. The circle was working!

Hoodwink jumped at the circle next, but stopped at the last moment. Turning, he leaned against a pillar with his new crown at a jaunty angle, and crossed his arms.

'*Go*,' the Professor yelled.

'Aw, come on,' the elf yelled back. 'How often do you get to watch a dragon explode?'

'Just go,' said the Professor, shoving the elf between the stones. He, too, vanished.

The Professor turned back, holding out a hand to Alfie. He was only a few feet away now, panting as he strained to push Betsy through the gold.

'Leave her, Rupert,' the Professor shouted. '*Drop her, you silly sprout.*'

'Nearly there,' Alfie gasped. With a final effort, he shoved the moped between the stones.

Then, three things happened at once.

One: Alfie bent down and scooped up a crash helmet full of gold.

Two: the Professor grabbed him by the jumper, and jumped backwards, dragging Alfie with him.

Three: the dragon finally exploded.

The force of the explosion flung Alfie between the two giant stones. He felt the universe open up. Finally, he was on his way back to his mum. Joy surged through him.

And then pain.

Alfie crashed to a cold floor with Betsy beneath him.

Opening his eyes with a groan, he immediately panicked. He couldn't see strange galaxies swirling overhead, let alone any brains in jars. There was only darkness: hot, sticky, smelly, *heavy* darkness. Something had gone wrong. He opened his mouth to shout in frustration and found he couldn't breathe. What weird world had he travelled to now? How many trillions of light years was he from his mum?

In darkness, he heard the word 'heave'.

With a revolting squelching sound, Alfie's fellow questers lifted a chunk of smoking dragon off him. Dripping gore, but still clutching a motorcycle helmet full of gold to his chest, Alfie blinked up into a circle of faces. Above them

brains sat in pink liquid, doing
absolutely nothing in a mysterious manner.

Sir Brenda spoke first, her
words translated by the Professor's
device.

'If you're ever looking for a job,
I'd like to offer you the position of
Dragon Slayer at Sir Brenda's Valiant
Quests,' she said Prince Hoodwink lifted an
eyebrow. 'The only person *ever* to slay a dragon,'
he said. 'Shame you're all covered in guts and yuk.
Not a good look. But maybe I won't put that
in the song. No, on second thoughts I
will put that in the song.'

Even Derek was looking at him with respect in
her eyes. 'Not pathetic. Not pathetic at all,' she said,
giving Alfie a nod of approval.

'Are you quite all right, Rupert?' said the
Professor.

With a sigh, Alfie sat up,
unwinding a length of dragon intestine
that had wrapped itself around his
neck. 'Ew,' he said, wrinkling his nose. 'I killed the

dragon. Does this mean I have to marry the almost lovely Daphne?'

CHAPTER TWENTY-NINE
THE BRAIN-LINED
PATH TO HOME

Sometimes Lady Luck smiles and after a quest filled with danger, she finally gave Alfie and his companions a break. The dragon's circle dropped them beside jar number 2,698,787,149,251. It wasn't as lucky as finding themselves next to jar 2,698,787,238,969, but was a lot better than—say—jar 1. As he poured the last of the petrol into Betsy's tank and straightened bent handlebars, Alfie calculated they were about fifty miles from where they needed to be. It could have been a lot further.

For the last time, the five questers set out together on the final stretch of the path that led to home, to Skingrath (hopefully), and to a modelling job. With only a straight, brain-lined road before them they chatted happily about Alfie's victory.

'Thanks for—you know—saving our lives Hoodwink,' said Alfie. 'When you came out of the tunnel shooting all those arrows, I mean. I thought you were hiding?'

'Got bored,' shrugged the elf.

'And you were *amazing*, Derek,' Alfie continued. 'The way you jumped onto the dragon's neck was just *awesome*.'

To his complete lack of surprise, Derek grunted.

'But we really all owe our lives to *you*, Rupert,' beamed the Professor. 'Very clever of you using the translator like that. Brain the size of a family hatchback, eh? Just the sort of young man the UCC needs if it's going to survive.'

'It was a shame to kill such a magnificent creature,' Alfie sighed. 'But at least the people of Verminium are safe now, and we've got all this gold. Minus fifty percent for Sir Brenda, of course.'

'Oh yes, I'd forgotten about that,' said Sir Brenda with a grin. 'Herkleton *will* be pleased. If you wouldn't mind writing a review for Sir Brenda's

Valiant Quests—just saying what a great time you've had—we could put it in the shop window. It would really help bring in the customers.'

'I think we can do better than that, can't we Professor?' said Alfie, giving the crash helmet a shake and setting the gold jingling. 'What do you say? Shall we tell Wrenchpenny he can't demolish the UCC headquarters after all? Start sending Sir Brenda more customers?'

'Wrenchpenny,' the Professor snarled. 'That oaf.' He fell silent.

Alfie smiled, waiting, as Betsy sped past brains. He could almost see the cogs in the Professor's own brain whirring. The old man's nose wrinkled as if he was imagining someone else wiping his bottom for him, which, in fact, is *exactly* what he was imagining. Alfie counted: one, two, three . . .

'I've been . . . ah . . . thinking about your plans for the Unusual Cartography Club, young Rupert,' said the Professor.

'Oh, really?' said Alfie.

'I believe I've been an old fool,' the Professor continued. 'Stuck in my ways, eh? It would be good to see some life back in the old place. People using the circle again. Having a jolly time on their holidays. Buckets and spades. Drinks by the pool. Flip-flops. Sun cream. That sort of thing. So if you're still interested you could become a full member of the Unusual Cartography Club or—should I say— the Unusual Travel Agency. We'd consider your apprenticeship served. You've more than earned it. As a full member you'd be entitled to rooms at headquarters. It's a big place so use as many as you like. Bring your mum, too, if she'd like to open a *gift shop*.' The Professor forced the last two words through gritted teeth then looked Derek up and down. 'And the UCC always has a place for brave adventurers if young Derek wants to join as well,' he said.

Alfie looked at Derek. 'What do you think?' he said. 'We can send you back to your people or you could stay. Maybe we'll find Skingrath one day.'

Derek shrugged.

'She says we'll think about it,' Alfie told the Professor.

'Oh, ah. I was hoping you'd . . .'

'We've thought about it, and the answer is *yes*.'
Alfie grinned. 'Oh, look, jar 2,698,787,238,969, steer
slightly to the left, Professor.'

Betsy wheezed and backfired her way between
two stone columns in the basement of Number
Four, Wigless Square. As the Professor applied the
brakes, her engine coughed once and died. The last
drop of petrol Alfie had packed almost three weeks
earlier had gone.

Leaping off the moped, Alfie danced around the circle, twice, before remembering something. 'What time is it?' he yelped. 'What *day* is it?'

The Professor checked an old grandfather clock that showed the time on thirty-six planets. 'Same day we left. Four-thirty in the afternoon,' he said. Digging around in an inside pocket, he pulled out a handful of notes and coins, dropping them into Alfie's hand. 'I hereby declare this quest complete, which means I owe you forty-nine pounds and forty-nine pence. We were supposed to check some other worlds too, if you remember, but as you've been such an excellent helper, Rupert, you may take the rest of the day off.'

'It's Alfie, Professor,' said Alfie.

'Alfie Professor? Inventor of the cheese grater? Where?' said the Professor, looking around.

'No, *I'm* Alfie,' said Alfie. 'My name is *Alfie*, not Rupert.'

'Is it? Is it *really*?' The Professor blinked. 'Why on Earth didn't you say so, Rupert?'

From above came the sound of someone hammering at the door. 'That will be Wrenchpenny,'

Alfie sighed. 'If you don't mind, Professor, I'm going to leave him to you. Can I take another Universal Translator? Thanks.'

Alfie rummaged in a drawer, and hung another translator around his neck. He passed one to Derek, too, then quickly threw one at Sir Brenda and another at Prince Hoodwink.

'Do I have to wear this?' asked the elf prince, turning it this way and that. 'Only it's not very stylish is it?'

'It's not *supposed* to be stylish,' Alfie told him. 'You don't have to wear it if you don't want to. I don't care, but no one on Earth will be able to understand you. That would be nice for them but might make it difficult getting a modelling job. I've got to go now. Goodbye, Sir Brenda. I'm sure we'll be seeing you soon but say "hi" to Herkleton for me. Come on Derek.'

'Off to see your mum, eh?' the Professor chuckled. 'Don't worry, I'll take care of Wrenchpenny. I've been looking forward to it, as a matter of fact. Give him a piece of my mind, eh? Send him off with a flea in his ear. Is it a flea, or a heron? I never can remember . . .'

'You know the ugly boy's already gone, right?' Hoodwink interrupted, winding the handle on his translator. 'So, Wanja-face, which way to the modelling agency?'

CHAPTER THIRTY
FEET MADE OF KITTENS

Alfie flung open the UCC's front door. For a second he drank in the sight of the city outside: *his* dirty, smelly, greasy, noisy city. The odd collection of buildings clustered around Wigless Square was exactly as he had left them. The windows were still boarded up or broken. The battered Rolls-Royce was still parked halfway up the pavement. In the middle of the central garden the statue was wearing a white hat made of pigeon droppings. And, once again, Wrenchpenny was on the doorstep.

'Who is this?' growled Derek. 'He has the face of a Despicable Scavenbator. Shall I pull his spine out and beat him round the head with it?'

'No time. We're going shopping,' Alfie replied. 'Hello, Mr Wrenchpenny. The Professor will be with you in a second. He said something about stuffing a heron in your ear. Good luck with that. Come *on*, Derek.' Grabbing her by the wrist, he pulled her into the street leaving the confused Wrenchpenny on the doorstep.

Behind them, the Professor's voice bellowed, 'What do you think of this then eh, Wrenchpenny you foul clot? It's a crash helmet brimming with gold. Enough to fix up the old place don't you think, you miserable thieving worm?'

★ ⋆ ☆

Two hours and forty-seven minutes after Betsy had puttered back into the basement at Number Four, Wigless Square, Alfie's mum opened the door of their tiny flat.

She was immediately hit by a tornado screaming, '*MUUUUUUUM*!'

'Um . . . hi,' gasped Alfie's mum, returning the hug. 'I missed you, too. But you're going to squeeze my lungs right out through my bottom. Could you ease up a bit?'

'No,' said Alfie, hugging harder. 'I don't think I could.'

'OK then, but my feet are killing me. Hang on tight, I'm going to the sofa.'

Reluctantly, Alfie let her go. He beamed up into her face. 'I thought I'd never see you again,' he croaked.

This is where things started to get weird for Alfie's mum. She started well, saying, 'Long day? Me too . . .' then stopped as her eyes travelled over her son. 'Hang on . . .' she continued, 'you're *filthy*. Why are you covered in soot and blood? Why are there twigs in your hair? Why have you got a tiny gramophone hanging around your neck? One of your *eyebrows* is missing, did you know that? And you look like you slept in a combine harvester. There's a piece of kidney stuck to your jumper. Alfie, what *happened* to you? And what's that *awful* smell?'

'Oh yes, I nearly forgot. Mum, meet Derek,' said Alfie, stepping aside to reveal the Skingrathian girl behind him.

'Derek? *Really*?' said his mother, looking Derek up and down. By now Derek's furs were glued to her with old sweat and muck. It looked like she'd need a hammer and chisel to get undressed. 'Interesting outfit, sweetie. Nice . . . um . . . stinking animal skins.'

'Thank . . . you,' said Derek. Alfie was impressed. She had hardly choked on the words at all. In another surprising first, she also looked . . . odd. At first, Alfie couldn't decide what was wrong with her. Then it hit him: she was *shy*. The Skingrathian warrior squirmed like she needed the toilet. She stood, looking up at his mum through matted hair, twisting her fingers together.

'You smell of fish guts, Alfie's mum,' Derek continued. 'Do you like fish guts? I decorated my hair with fish guts last winter. I still have some in here. Would you like them? They are dry now but still quite ker-twa-bing-bing muffin.' She began fiddling with her dreadlocks.

'It's sweet of you, but no thanks,' said Alfie's mum. She gave Alfie a look that said *What*?

'I think she said the fish guts are still quite tasty,'

said Alfie, helpfully, while he wound the Universal Translator. 'Though you made the right choice if you want my opinion. If they've been in her hair they're probably not good to eat.'

'*Alfie*,' said his mum. There was a slight note of warning in her voice. 'You haven't answered my questions. Who *is* this person? What's going on?'

'I also have a squirrel brain in here somewhere,' Derek mumbled, still fussing with her hair.

'Derek's an alien,' Alfie explained. 'Well, she's human but from a different planet. Outlandish, it's called. It's on the other side of the universe somewhere. She's going to live with us.'

'Alfie, we don't have room,' yelped his mum. 'Where's she going to . . . what are you doing? What's happening now?'

Alfie was rummaging around down the front of his trousers. 'Not *here*. We're not living *here*. We're moving to Wigless Square. Oh, and I got you a present and you can quit working at the fish market. I need you to open a gift shop. T-shirts, mugs, guide books, elf shampoo: that sort of thing. And I got you this,' said Alfie, pulling an egg-sized diamond from his trousers like a magician pulling a rabbit from his hat. 'Ta da!' he added. 'We are no longer poor.'

Alfie's mum stared at the jewel in her son's hand. 'Is that a *diamond*?' she croaked. 'Alfie, my boy, what *have* you been up to?'

'It's not *stolen*,' Alfie told her. 'Well, a *little* bit stolen but it's all right because I killed the original owner. Blew him up. *Boom*! Like that. Chunks of flesh *everywhere*. You should have seen his face! That's why I'm covered in blood and kidney.'

'*Alfie*!' There was a definite note of warning in his mother's voice now.

Alfie took a breath, going over what he'd just said in his head. 'That might have sounded bad,' he admitted.

'Your son is a mighty warrior,' Derek chipped in. 'We have adventured together across Outlandish and now, together, we seek Skingrath, the three-headed flame-haired god of war—'

'I was hoping we could have a break before we go looking for Skingrath,' Alfie interrupted.

Derek ignored him. 'We shall seek Him in His land of burning pain and infinite misery and then—'

Seeing the look on his mother's face, Alfie interrupted. '*Derek*, you're not helping. Let *me* explain.'

'Ha, you slay one dragon and now you think you are Under-Sixteens Explaining Champion,' hissed Derek. 'But you explain like you fight: *badly*.'

'I saved your life,' Alfie replied. 'You could try being nice.'

'I am being . . . *nice*,' said Derek, through her teeth. 'Did you not hear me tell of your great deeds?'

'Blah blah blah Skingrath, is what I heard,' said Alfie. 'As usual.'

'We will settle this like warriors,' she snarled, crouching. 'By wrestling. To the death.'

'*Enough*!' shouted Alfie's mum. 'No one is wrestling anyone else to the death. There isn't enough room in here. You. *Derek*. Where are your parents?'

'I have no parents,' said Derek.

Alfie blinked. 'But you said the woman who gave birth to you sent you into the wilderness.'

'She did,' Derek replied. 'And while I was fighting for my life the high priest sent her off to war. My father, too. They were both killed. *That* is the reason I seek Skingrath. Not to bring word of him to my people but to find my parents. For it is written that after death all warriors will be reborn into his world of fire.' She scowled. 'There. Now you know the truth. I am weak. All along I just wanted to see *my* mum, too.'

For a moment there was a stunned silence.

Alfie broke it. 'Oh Derek,' he threw his arms around her shaking shoulders. Seeing the expression on her face, he added, 'This is called a hug, it's supposed to help.'

'It . . . it . . . *does*,' said Derek. 'A little.'

'Oooookay,' said Alfie's mum, clapping her hands. 'I don't understand any of this but before anything else happens we're *all* going to have a shower. Not at the same time, obviously. That would be weird. Then—and *only* then—you are *both* going to explain to me what happened in the twelve hours since I left for work this morning. Is that understood?'

'Actually, it's been almost three weeks since you left for work,' said Alfie.

'Alfie,' said his mum, sounding firm. 'You get in the shower first. I want to talk to . . . Derek? You said your name was Derek, right? *Really* Derek?'

Alfie left the Universal Translator on the coffee table and took three steps to the bathroom of their tiny flat. Behind him, he heard his mum say, 'So, Derek, tell me—who looks after you?'

'Me,' said Derek. 'What's a shower?'

'We'll come to that very soon. Very soon indeed. First, let me get this straight. *No one* looks after you? No one at all? How long has this been going on?'

'Since I was six winters old.'

'Well *that's* not right, is it?' said Alfie's mum. 'We'll have to do something about that.'

As Alfie turned on the shower he heard the sound of wrapping paper being torn. 'A Sole Sensation 6000. Oh my,' said his mum.

Alfie smiled. Plan C had worked.

★ ⋆ ★

When everyone was clean and no one smelled of fish guts or dragon smoke or mouldy rabbit skin, Alfie sipped a mug of hot chocolate and stared at Derek.

Alfie's mum had turned the radio on, quietly, and Derek's foot tapped along to the latest sounds of Jamie Fringe. She was wearing a pair of Alfie's jeans and a charity shop t-shirt. It had an arrow printed on it and words that read 'I'm With This Moron. Please Help.' For the first time ever, Alfie had seen her laugh out loud when he told her what it meant, and—since then—she had been careful to sit so the arrow was pointing to Alfie.

Budget shampoo had done its best. Her dreadlocks were less smelly and had been tied back behind her head. Her face was no longer covered with muck and paint.

Alfie smiled again. He was home. Derek hadn't really found what she was looking for, yet. But his mum had made it quite clear that she'd be looking after the Skingrathian girl for as long as she needed looking after, so maybe she'd found something to be going on with. And maybe, Alfie thought, he *had* found a sister.

Mums being mums, Alfie's was way more pleased with the foot spa than she was with a diamond worth millions, which sparkled on the kitchen table, completely forgotten. She wiggled her toes in warm water while vibrating toe-polishers did their happy work. 'Oh, that's *good*,' she sighed. 'That is *soooo* good. It's like my feet are made out of kittens. A Sole Sensation 6000. Who'd have thought I'd ever own a Sole Sensation 6000? Best. Son. *Ever*. But they cost a hundred and forty-nine pounds and ninety-nine pence. How did you ever manage to afford it?'

'I've been playing the stock market,' said Alfie. 'At the library.'

'You've been doing *what*?'

'But I still didn't have quite enough money, so this morning—three weeks ago—I answered a job advert in the newspaper. Now I sort of have a new business to start . . .'

With Derek talking over him, and his mum putting a stop to any wrestling that threatened to break out, Alfie told her everything. By the end, his mum could have chosen to think that her son had gone completely bonkers. But she was Alfie's mum so, instead, she just said 'Wow.'

THE UNUSUAL TRAVEL AGENCY

A UNIVERSE OF SURPRISES AWAITS!

Discover Ancient Whodat and the Curious Monument of Pharaoh Bad-Hat IV

PLUS

Discover your future with the Mystical Serpent of Nerwong Nerwong Plinky-Plonk

Year-round skiing on Planet Brrrrrchillyoutagain

AND MUCH MUCH MORE

SUN, SEA, AND SAND ON BLYSSS:

SEE INSIDE FOR OUR THREE-WEEK LUNCH-BREAK SPA OFFERS!

WELCOME, travellers, to the Unusual Travel Agency's Winter Collection. Whether you're looking for culture, fine food, relaxation, or having your brain spring-cleaned by a friendly Limpatian Cranium Toad, we've got the holiday for you. Within these pages you'll find destinations for every taste at a price to suit every pocket. From backpacking in the Eccentrika, where locals welcome visitors with open feelers, to luxury hovership cruises round the cloud cities of Vertigo Three, you'll be amazed at our intergalactic tours. And don't forget, we're adding new destinations every day, so if you can't find the planet that's right for you our experienced team will go out and discover it!

TUBEWORMS: the only way to travel through Perkhole—hire yours today from Twerpz Tubeworms.

- -

Help yourself pack before you go away! On planet RUBBER SWIMMING-HAT IV time moves backwards. Book your holiday now and a younger, fitter you will return before you've even left.

- -

At TWERKERZ NIGHTCLUB our open-air dance floor is lit by the supernovas of the Volatile Sector. Party the night away under a trillion exploding stars!

MEET OUR

PROFESSOR PEWSLEY BOWELL-MOUVEMONT

Professor Bowell-Mouvemont is President of The Unusual Travel Agency and its chief map-maker. He helped compile *The Cosmic Atlas* as well as writing several books, including *Where the Heck Am I Now?*, *Around The Universe in a Corset*, and *Incredibly Dangerous Intergalactic Travel For the Elderly*.

ALFIE FLEET

Vice-President of the UTA, Alfie is also known as 'Dragonslayer' or 'that twazzock who blew up all the treasure in Mount Gallyvant'. The agency's most popular guide, he has survived many tours of Outlandish with only minor injuries, lice infestations, and a variety of stomach parasites.

HUNTER-OF-THE-VICIOUS SPINY-DEREKO-BEAST

Another popular tour guide, Derek has been described by the UTA's customers as 'a bit scary but useful in a fight'. She is our expert on hunting, fishing, mountain biking, and threatening behaviour.

TOUR GUIDES

SIR BRENDA OF VERMINIUM

Outlandish's greatest hero, and now Queen of Verminium, Sir Brenda provides our clients with amazing quests and is the author of *Magical Beasts and How to Slaughter Them*.

PRINCE HOODWINK

Who better to guide you on your travels than a gorgeous elven prince? Well, almost anyone really. He's extremely annoying.

GERALD TEETHCRUSHER

The 'faymus' Gerald Teethcrusher is the Unusual Travel Agency's chief restaurant critic and guide to the latest fashions in leather pants.

BLYSSS

A tropical world of islands, three suns, and the only planet in the universe where the sunlounger was invented before the wheel, Blysss is the perfect planet for anyone looking for a really good tan. Strict local laws mean that you'll be held down in the arrivals area by locals who will forcibly bead your hair, but after that it's fun all the way!

WHERE TO STAY . . .

PARADYSSS BAY ★★★★

Probably the finest resort in the universe, Paradysss Bay offers ocean views and non-stop, round-the-clock happiness. All rooms come with flower-strewn hot springs, kitten baskets, and a butler who will bring you drinks and win the lottery for you while you relax.

THANK GOODNESS IT'S BEACHCRUSHERS ★

Thank Goodness it's Beachcrushers is a falling-down shack that offers guests all the hospitality they've come to expect from Gerald Teethcrusher's chain of hotels and restaurants: none at all. Thankfully, there are no fleas on Blysss but visitors can expect their bed to be infested with crabs.

ANCIENT WHODAT

Travel in style on the River of Stinking Lilies and walk among the weird monuments lining its banks. Elsewhere in the universe, ancient rulers built their burial temples in the shape of pyramids, but on Whodat the pharaohs chose to have themselves buried in vast buildings shaped like backsides. During your tour you'll be invited to watch the ancient, torchlight 'Mooning the Gods' ceremony at the famous monument of Pharaoh Bad-Hat IV. This ceremony is not suitable for younger children.

WHERE TO STAY . . .

THE HAPPY GRAVE ☆☆☆

Once the final resting place of Pharaoh Spoon XV, this old
monument has been cleaned up a bit, and the worst of the cobwebs
are now gone. You will still find the mummified body of the old
pharaoh in the hotel though. He is now the receptionist.

THANK GOODNESS IT'S BOTTOMCRUSHER'S ☆

Do *not* stay here.

AN **ALL NEW** OUTLANDISH ADVENTURE FROM

SIR BRENDA'S
VALIANT QUESTS . . .

DEATH ROCK MINE

Even the youngest members of YOUR family will love this
kid-friendly quest. Starting just outside the town of Witch's
Grim, you'll descend with Sir Brenda into the crumbling mines
where grisly undead lurk around every corner. Battle your way
through the tunnels where murderous deathtraps are waiting
to go off, before diving into the Vortex of Pain to enter the
Realm of Brutality. Here, the kiddies can make friends with
giant skeleton ants with razor-sharp claws at the Petting Zoo.
At the end of the quest the whole family will love facing the
skull-headed sorcerer known as 'The Devourer of Flesh' in an
epic battle, before facing mortal danger again with lunch at the
Teethcrusher Café.

DON'T FORGET TO VISIT OUR GIFT SHOP

T-SHIRTS & MUGS

I ♥ BOWELL-MOUVEMONT

DEMON TOENAIL

OUTLANDISH WORLD TOUR

I went to Fank Goodness it's Teefcrushers and all I got Woz Fleeez.

ACKNOWLEDGEMENTS

MAHOOOSIVE THANKS to a great bunch of people: The prodigiously talented Chris Mould; the editorial, sales, and marketing teams at Oxford University Press who all showed me a fun time, but especially Kathy Webb, Debbie Sims, and Rob Lowe, who made this book read brilliantly and look amazing; and my one-in-a-million agent, Penny Holroyde, who is also a proper mate. My offspring—Maia, Buffy, and Sam—tried a little bit not to disturb me while I was writing so I suppose I should thank them too. Last, and most, never-ending gratitude to my astonishing wife, Emma, whose patience is Olympic standard.

I love you.

Mart x

MARTIN HOWARD

Martin Howard is a raffle-winning author who took first prize (a girl's bike) at the Holtspur Middle School Summer Fete in 1986. Although he makes fun of fantasy and sci-fi books he is a massively nerdy fan of both, and likes a good laugh, too. Martin prefers to be called Mart, talks in his sleep, enjoys toast, and lives in France with his wife, three children, and a grumpy dog called Licky.

CHRIS MOULD

Chris is an award-winning illustrator who went to art school at 16. A sublime draughtsman with a penchant for the gothic, he has illustrated the gamut from picture books and young fiction, to theatre posters and satirical cartoons for national newspapers. He lives in Yorkshire with his wife, has two grown-up daughters, and when he's not drawing and writing, you'll find him... actually, he's never not drawing or writing.

Ready for more incredible adventures? Try these!

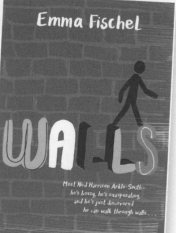